She was getting to him...

It was becoming harder and harder to distract Maggie Brown from her goal. Or maybe that was because Ben was finding her equally distracting. He could smell the soap on her skin, the shampoo in her hair as it blew dry in the breeze. He could smell temptation and sin on the air. But he couldn't smell redemption.

There was only one way to shut Maggie up, make her forget about her sister, her questions, her hostility. One way to turn her from a terrier with a bone to a soft, melting mass of femininity. He could take her to bed. And Ben didn't doubt for one minute she'd let him do it, against her better judgment.

Welcome, newest eHarlequin.com member!

As you know, when it comes to romance, no one compares to Harlequin. When it comes to romance online, eHarlequin.com is unequivocally the best Internet destination for romantic escape. These 2 FREE books have been written exclusively for eHarlequin.com and are available only from www.eHarlequin.com. They are our way of saying welcome to romance online!

Be sure to explore all of www.eHarlequin.com. As a member you are now eligible to participate in all eHarlequin.com promotions and events. The site is divided into three main channels:

❤ **Your Romantic Books** is the place to read, write, and shop. You can purchase Harlequin, Silhouette, MIRA, and Steeple Hill books at great discounts. Read online serials written exclusively for eHarlequin.com, vote in our Interactive Novel, and find fascinating interviews with all your favorite authors. Have a Heart-to-Heart with other members and authors in our community, or write the next chapter of the Writing Round Robin.

❤ **Your Romantic Life** features expert advice on romance and relationships, and how-to guides for making your love life richer and more exciting, such as Flirting 101. Included are features such as Recipes for Romance, and Dr. Romance—our romance expert who answers a new relationship question each week. Or, discuss your romance dilemmas with other members in our Tales of the Heart message board.

❤ **Your Romantic Escapes** promises to be the ultimate in online indulgence, featuring Lovescopes that forecast love and passion for you, romantic travel destinations, romantic movie reviews, and interactive games, such as Six Degrees of On-Screen Kisses (a fun celebrity kissing game).

I'm sure you'll enjoy every minute of the time you spend on www.eHarlequin.com. We aim to satisfy all your online romance desires.

Happy reading!

Pam Laycock

Executive Vice President, eHarlequin.com

ANNE STUART

The Fall of Maggie Brown

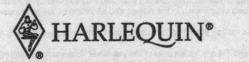

TORONTO • NEW YORK • LONDON
AMSTERDAM • PARIS • SYDNEY • HAMBURG
STOCKHOLM • ATHENS • TOKYO • MILAN • MADRID
PRAGUE • WARSAW • BUDAPEST • AUCKLAND

ISBN 0-373-15329-5

THE FALL OF MAGGIE BROWN

Copyright © 2000 by Anne Kristine Stuart Ohlrogge

Dear Reader,

When the editors at Harlequin asked me to write a book exclusively for the Internet subscribers, I jumped at the chance. I'm a complete Internet junkie, and would rather spend all my shopping and research time chained to my computer, so I thought writing a book available only through the Internet would be perfect for me.

And I loved the challenge—it was a length I'd never written, and the time was tight, so I had no choice but to dive right into it, immersing myself completely. Since that's the way I prefer to write, it was a match made in heaven.

I had a marvelous time with uptight Maggie and swashbuckling Ben. I hope you do, too.

Cheers,

Anne Stuart

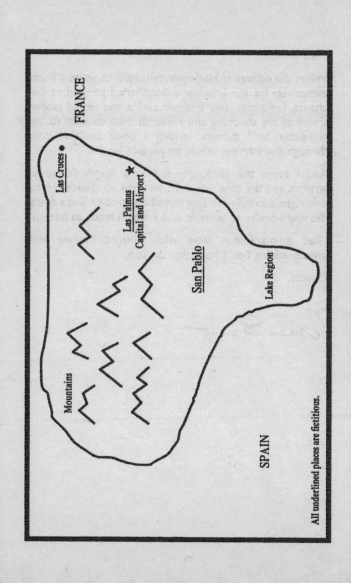

All underlined places are fictitious.

CAST OF CHARACTERS

Maggie Brown—A repressed banker from Philadelphia.

Ben Frazer—A soldier-of-fortune type living in San Pablo.

Stella Brown—Maggie's feckless, irresponsible twin sister.

Delia Brown—Their feckless, irresponsible mother.

Ramon Morales de Lorca y Antonio, The Professor—Leader of the opposition party.

Generalissimo Cabral—Dictator of San Pablo.

Elena—Owner of a local hotel, and Ben's former lover.

Salazar—A San Pablo crime boss.

El Gallito Loco—Cabral's assassin and Ben's nemesis.

CHAPTER ONE

MAGGIE BROWN WALKED into the seedy, run-down bar with the no-nonsense stride of someone who was at ease with the world. It was all an act, of course. She wouldn't have been comfortable walking alone into a bar at the Waldorf Astoria, much less in a low-rent dive in Las Cruces, San Pablo, a tiny country somewhere between Spain and France, just to the right of Andorra in more ways than one. Had it been up to Maggie, she would have been safe at home in Philadelphia, spending her days in peaceful monotony, dividing her time between her job at the bank and her tasteful apartment.

She should have known her life wouldn't stay peaceful for long, not when she considered the family she'd been born into.

They'd always been evenly matched. Maggie and her father, Frank, the sane, levelheaded sensible ones. And Maggie's twin sister, Stella, and their flighty mother, Delia, both of them without enough common sense to come in out of the rain. Throughout her twenty-eight years Maggie had helped her father look out for the rest of their impractical family, and since her father's death two years ago she'd done what she could on her own.

Which brought her to Las Cruces, San Pablo, on a damp autumn day, searching for her errant twin and hoping to God her mother would hold on long enough for Maggie to bring the stray home.

Delia was dying. Delia often said she was dying, being possessed of a strong imagination, but this time Maggie was ready to believe it. Her mother had taken to her bed some three months ago, growing paler and weaker and murmuring mysteriously of doctors' appointments, until she'd announced she wanted to see Stella just once before she died.

And Maggie, dutiful, responsible daughter that she was, had taken a leave of absence from the bank, packed nonwrinkling clothes in her lightweight carry-on and taken the next flight to San Pablo.

Stella was as emotional, changeable, impractical and breathless as a butterfly, flitting from man to man with an innocent disregard of commitment and the future. Not that sensible Maggie had found anyone to build a future with. But at least she didn't go flying off at the drop of a hat, certain she was in love two or three times a year.

This latest one had lasted longer, but Maggie didn't hold out any hope for permanence. She doubted Stella knew the meaning of the word. It had been just over a year ago when Stella, living in New York and making a marginal living modeling for art classes, had met the mysterious Ramon and fallen in love. And for once in her life, instead of boring Maggie with endless details, she'd been suspiciously silent.

Leaving Maggie with the dread suspicion that she'd fallen in love with a terrorist.

It wasn't that great a leap. According to Stella's sketchy details, Ramon was part of a group of patriots trying to free the tiny country of San Pablo from its oppressive dictatorship, and he'd been in New York to raise money for the cause. A cause Stella had thrown herself into with her usual wholehearted enthusiasm, and when Ramon had returned to his beleaguered country Stella had, of course, gone with him.

Three postcards in the last year. Three torn, stained, battered postcards from the idyllic, tiny country of San Pablo, with nothing more than a scrawled greeting in Stella's characteristic hand.

No mention of where she was, nor of Ramon. Nor of anything at all.

The last postcard, sent sometime in the spring, had shown a religious procession winding through a small mountain town. The town of Las Cruces, which looked a lot better on a gaudily colored postcard than it did in the dismal light of day.

The gloomy bar was even less prepossessing. It was raining lightly, and Maggie had left her umbrella back in the tiny hotel room, an almost unprecedented oversight on her part. It shouldn't have surprised her—she was anxious and worried and jet-lagged. But she wasn't the type to forget essentials.

She squared her shoulders, trying to summon forth the vision of her stern, no-nonsense father, and she ran a hand over her damp, tangled hair. The place was almost deserted. An old man stood behind the bar, and there were several silent customers scattered among the handful of tables, all watching her out of still, hostile eyes. In one corner a bundle of rags shifted, drawing her gaze to the bowed head, the long, tangled hair, the scruffy cheek. And then she reached the bar, her high heels clicking on the rough wood flooring, like tiny taps.

"Good afternoon, *señor*," she greeted the bartender. The man didn't move for a moment, then leaned forward and spat on the floor.

The woman at the hotel had assured her that the bartender spoke English, and that he would know who could help her find her sister. If he'd understood her greeting he was making no effort to show it. He leaned back, crossing his arms over his burly, none-too-clean chest, and looked at her.

"Señora Campos sent me here," Maggie continued gamely, wondering if she ought to dig in the huge bag she carried with her for her trusty phrase book. "I'm looking for my sister, and the *señora* said you might be able to help."

He didn't even blink. He was quite old, she realized, and his leathery skin was lizardlike. "I'm looking for some information," she added, trying to keep the note of desperation out of her voice. When she'd called her mother last night to report her singular lack of success there'd been no answer, and while Maggie had never been one to panic, it was almost impossible to shake a sense of nagging dread. What if her mother died when both her daughters were missing? Who was there to be with her, get her to the hospital if need be?

A dozen or more devoted friends, she reminded herself. Delia Rathburn Brown had an uncanny ability to gather people around her who had nothing better to do than look after her. She didn't need either of her daughters to see to her well-being.

The bartender leaned forward, staring at her. Maggie held her own, with the simple assurance that she posed no threat, and indeed, little interest, to anyone.

"My sister…" she began again. What the hell was the Spanish word for sister? She could remember French, and even Italian, but Spanish was eluding her completely. And besides, the people of San Pablo had their own dialect that was almost as far removed from Spanish as the Basque language.

He said something, almost a bark of sound, and she stared at him. "I beg your pardon?"

"Frazer," the man said a little more distinctly. He jerked his head toward the pile of old clothes. "He'll help you. If you've got the price."

Maggie looked toward the rags, watching them move, slowly gathering themselves into the form of a man. He rose, and in the darkness he seemed enormously tall next to the short bartender, next to her own five feet four inches. He had a hat pulled down over his eyes, two or three days' growth of beard, long tangled hair brushing his shoulders and some moth-eaten old poncho covering up dun-colored clothes. She couldn't see his face in the dim afternoon light, and she wasn't sure she wanted to.

The bartender spoke rapidly in his oddly accented Spanish, and after a few words Maggie gave up her futile attempt to follow along. He was talking about her, and she had a good guess it wasn't very complimentary, but there was nothing she could do about it. Not until the lanky bundle of rags decided to speak.

When he did it was in the same Spanish, though his accent was even odder. He turned his head and glanced at her from under the brim of his hat, and Maggie resisted the impulse to yank it from his head in frustration. "Miguel here says you're looking for your sister." His voice was a low, husky drawl, with a rough tinge to it.

"If you'd been listening you'd know that I said the same thing," she said briskly. "My sister came to San Pablo a little over a year ago and apart from a few postcards we haven't heard from her. I want to make sure she's okay."

He nodded, though she suspected it was more to signify understanding than agreement. "And what will you do when you find her?" he asked. "Drag her back home like a bad little girl?"

His voice sent odd little shivers down her spine. She couldn't even see what he looked like, a fact which annoyed her, and he was too tall. She didn't like men who loomed over her.

"Our mother is dying," she said flatly. "She wants to know that Stella is safe before she goes."

"In which case wouldn't you be better off not finding her? If your mother is waiting to die until you find out what happened to your sister then obviously she'd stay alive until you do. And what if you find she's been murdered by bandits? Wouldn't dear old mom be better off not knowing?"

Maggie just stared at him in disbelieving horror. "Bandits?"

"Not that there are many nowadays. Most of them have joined Generalissimo Cabral's goon squad. But maybe you'd be much happier turning around and heading back to America and telling your mom that your sister will come home when she's good and ready."

Maggie took a deep breath. "I do thank you for your kind concern," she said icily, "but I wasn't asking for advice. I simply need to find my sister, and my reasons are none of your business and not up for discussion. I'm sure there'll be someone around here who can help me..."

She glanced behind her, at the men watching them. As if on cue they ducked their heads and concentrated on their drinks. The bartender had disappeared.

She looked back at him and he tipped the hat off his head so that she could see his eyes. Even in the darkness they were a bright, electric-blue, set in his unshaven, unfriendly, undeniably attractive face, and his mouth curved in a taunting, cynical grin.

"Honey," he drawled, "if you're looking for help, then I'm all you've got. Accept it."

She considered a defiant, thrilling response of "never!" She didn't say a word, simply looked him over slowly, from the top of his shaggy head to the scuffed boots on his feet. He was disreputable, probably drunk and doubtless more trouble than she'd ever handled in her life.

However, she was very good at handling trouble, and she wasn't about to back down now. She needed to find her sister.

So she simply nodded. "All right," she said briskly. "Meet me at the hotel for dinner, and I'll tell you everything I know about my sister's disappearance."

"We haven't even discussed terms."

"We can discuss them over dinner. I'm very good at negotiating, Mr. Frazer. I'm sure we'll come to a mutual agreement."

He didn't look sure of any such thing, but he didn't argue. "I'll be there."

"Seven o'clock," she said. "I imagine you'll want to...freshen up a bit."

"I'll be sure and powder my nose," he drawled. "You want me to bring flowers?"

"Just your lovely self, Mr. Frazer. And be assured, I have no problem paying well for what I need."

"And you need me, honey. Have no doubt about that. You gonna tell me your name?"

"Brown. Maggie Brown."

"Miss or Mrs.?"

"Ms."

"I don't come from the South, sugar. It's one or the other. You married?"

"No."

"Miss Brown, then," he said. "See you at seven." And he pushed by her, heading out into the afternoon drizzle without a backward glance.

She watched him go, frozen despite the thick, humid heat of the sultry afternoon. It wasn't until he'd disappeared that she let out her breath, surprised to discover she'd been holding it.

There was no sign of the bartender, and the other customers were studiously ignoring her. No one to answer questions, just the strange, hostile American who'd said he'd help her.

Did she believe him? Trust him? She didn't really have a choice. But damn Stella for putting her in this miserable position. This was the last time she was coming in search of her feckless twin. In the future she could look out for herself.

MISS MAGGIE BROWN was a pistol, Frazer thought, ambling along in the lightly falling rain. From the tips of her high-heeled shoes to the top of her slightly tousled brown hair she looked more at ease with a cell phone and a briefcase than in a run-down village in a country on the verge of revolution. She didn't want to be here, that much was certain, but she wasn't about to whine. She'd come here to do a job and by God she was going to do it, even if it meant she had to consort with riffraff like Ben Frazer.

And she had no earthly idea just how raffish he could be.

He was prepared to give Miss Maggie Brown a lesson in how the real world operated, as opposed to the civilized, rarefied stratum she usually inhabited. He'd take her money, he'd take her on a wild-goose chase and in the end she'd be poorer but wiser for the experience.

The one thing he wasn't going to do was take her to see her twin sister.

She didn't look much like Stella, despite the fact that she claimed they were twins. Stella was tall and buxom, and Maggie was short and slender. Not too slender, despite those baggy clothes. Stella was nothing less than a flaming, outrageous beauty, from the top of her undoubtedly dyed red mane to her perfect feet, while Maggie was paler, more subdued. A more refined, sophisticated taste, Ben thought. Fortunately he was more beer than champagne. He wasn't even tempted.

He rubbed a hand across his three-day growth of beard. Normally he was due for a shave, but nothing short of torture would make him take a razor to his stubble. Miss Maggie Brown was just going to have to appreciate her guide in all his rough-hewn glory. With any kind of luck he'd annoy her so much she wouldn't even realize he was taking her miles away from anyone who'd ever seen or heard of the magnificent Stella. By the time she realized she'd been had, it would be too late.

Too late to stop what had been in the works for far too long. The last thing anybody needed was a busybody poking her nose into San Pablo affairs, asking questions. The elections would be done in three days, and if all went well, a new order would be in charge. He wasn't about to let anything, including an unwanted American, jeopardize it.

Hell, it was nothing more than his duty to get rid of her. And on rare occasions, when he was bored and the price was right, he could be a very dutiful guy.

Besides he was curious. Beneath that staid appearance, was Maggie Brown anything like the wild and passionate Stella?

It might be interesting to find out.

THE MAN STOOD IN THE DOORWAY of the tumbledown house across from Señora Campos's prosperous little inn. He was the kind of man no one would look at twice—middle-aged, average height, a stocky build and a forgettable face. His very ordinariness had been his best stock in trade, one he'd used to advantage over the past thirty years.

It came in handy today, as he stood beneath the doorway, out of the way of the light mist, and watched the American woman enter the hotel. No one ever remembered him. He was the Everyman of San Pablo.

She'd been easy enough to follow—the stupid American had no idea anyone was interested in her whereabouts. No idea that she was unwittingly involved in the future of this country.

She would know when he killed her. He could give her that much, so she wouldn't die without knowing why. And he would do it as quickly and painlessly as possible. He liked to think of himself as a chivalrous man when it came to the ladies.

But for his old friend Ben Frazer he wasn't planning any such weakness. He owed him, owed him for the scar across his belly, owed him for the broken leg that still bothered him on occasion. With Ben Frazer, he had every intention of making it last.

In the meantime, though, he was content to watch. To keep his distance, to follow the girl as she led him to his ultimate prey. It was only his good fortune that Frazer came along with the package. A sign that the job was meant to be his. He'd take care of business. And then, when it came to Ben Frazer, he'd take care of pleasure.

El Gallito Loco, they called him. No one knew his real name, and he'd had so many he'd practically forgotten it himself. *El Gallito* served him well enough. If anyone was fool enough to think it was a harmless nickname, they would soon know otherwise.

In the meantime, all he had to do was watch and wait. Ben Frazer would take him straight to his prey.

And his own, exceedingly painful fate.

CHAPTER TWO

By THE TIME MAGGIE MADE IT to the little cantina attached to the run-down hotel she was ten minutes late, and the man named Frazer was already waiting for her. Maggie was never late for anything. If she had an appointment she always arrived at least fifteen minutes early and then had to circle the block several times until she could reasonably present herself.

But for some reason tonight she couldn't get ready. It wasn't as if she'd had a lot of choices in clothes. She carried a matching set of black and beige separates that would see her through any season and never needed ironing, and for dinner she always wore the plain black dress. For some reason it seemed a little too plain, a little too snug across the chest, a little too short, a little too everything. She wasted precious time trying everything else on in various combinations until she finally gave up and yanked the black dress on again.

At least the rain had stopped, leaving the air

sullen and humid. Her thick brown hair decided to stage a revolt against the damp climate, popping out of her smooth coif and curling around her face to make her look like a cherub. It eluded every attempt she made at taming it, and when she gave up and caught it in a scrunchie it immediately began to curl again. And she wasn't the type for curls.

Then she decided she looked too pale, and a woman needed makeup as a defense against the world, but for some reason the eyeliner and lipstick made her look like a wanton rather than a banker, so she scrubbed it off, only to discover that without it she looked seventeen and vulnerable.

It was lucky she wasn't an hour late.

He was already drinking when she arrived at the table, his long fingers wrapped around a bottle of beer. He looked up at her, hesitated just long enough to be rude and then slowly rose to his full height.

"Don't bother being polite," she said, taking the chair opposite him. "It doesn't suit you."

"I wouldn't want to spoil your preconceived notions," he drawled. "So when do you want to go?"

She blinked. She'd come prepared to handle this

meeting in a businesslike manner, and he'd already preempted her. "Go where?"

"Well, I kind of thought you were interested in finding your sister, but if you'd rather go back to my place…"

"You're obnoxious, Mr. Frazer. Did you know that?"

"Yes, ma'am. And the name's Ben, Maggie."

"The name's Ms. Brown, Mr. Frazer."

"You really want to waste time arguing about crap like that when your sister's missing and your mother's dying?" he said in his lazy voice.

Damned man. "I believe my mother is holding her own at the moment," she said stiffly. "And I don't think my sister's in any danger, she's just being thoughtless. But we need to come to an understanding if I'm going to hire your services."

He leaned back in his chair, arms folded across his chest, the picture of patience. He hadn't cleaned up much, though he'd lost the enveloping poncho that had covered him. He was wearing old, faded jeans, scruffy boots and a khaki shirt. He'd rolled up the sleeves, and the shirt was unbuttoned partway down his chest, exposing far too much tanned, golden skin. She was distracted, looking at that skin.

He hadn't shaved, but he'd tied back his ridiculously long hair, and he was watching her with a combination of amusement and patience, as if he were dealing with a cantankerous old woman. She didn't like being patronized.

"Well," he said finally.

"Well, what?"

"Are you going to keep staring at my chest or are you going to tell me how we're going to come to an understanding?"

"You could always button up your shirt instead of walking around like a male model."

"The buttons came off. You wanna sew them on for me?"

She pushed back from the table. "This isn't going to work."

"Quitter," he said, a note of laughter in his rough voice.

She'd been about to rise, but his taunt stopped her. "Why are you trying to annoy me, Mr. Frazer?"

"Because I want to see what you're made of. If we're going to go off into the hills looking for your sister I'll need to know what to expect. In case you hadn't realized it, this is a country on the verge of a revolution, and no one knows whether it'll be peaceful or not. There are bandits, revolutionaries, not to mention the army of the esteemed president,

Generalissimo Francisco Cabral. I'm not about to go into a dangerous situation like that without knowing what my backup is like.''

"Who says I'm going with you?'' she demanded, astonished.

"You thought you could just pack your bags and head back to the States, leaving me with the task? Sounds like an excellent idea. I appreciate your faith in me.''

"I have no faith in you, I don't even know you,'' she said irritably. "And I had no idea how you were planning to find her—you were the one who said you were my only hope. I expected I'd stay in town here and wait for you to get back to me. Maybe I could find some transportation to the capital city, make a few inquiries.''

He shook his head. "Easier said than done, sugar. No cars to rent, and you'd have to leave the way you came. By bus, I presume?''

Maggie shuddered. The endless bus ride north to Las Cruces from the tiny airport was possibly the worst five hours of her life.

Frazer's grin broadened. "I thought so. You just sit back, calm down, and I'll tell you what we're going to do, and what you're going to pay me to do it.''

"I beg your pardon..." she began, outrage stirring once more.

"Granted. Now be quiet and listen. Chances are your sister is somewhere in the southern part of San Pablo. That's where the revolutionaries are centered. This is a small country, and I hear a lot about what's going on. You said this was your twin sister? I haven't heard of any Americans who look like you, but there's been a tall, stacked redhead who's been seen near the lake region in the south—"

"That's Stella," she said grimly. "We're not identical." She waited for him to make some crack. If he'd heard about a tall redhead then he probably heard she was beautiful. She'd grown up in Stella's shadow, despite the fact that she was seventeen minutes older. She should be used to it by now.

"All right, we know where to start," he said, for once not baiting her. "Fact is, I've got a vehicle and fuel, something that isn't easily come by in San Pablo nowadays. I also know where to get more gas when we need it. The only other way you'd get to the lake region is to walk, and I don't see you tramping all those miles in those high heels."

She glanced down at her shoes. They were Fer-

ragamos, and she loved them. They made her
calves look long and slender, even made her feet
look sexy. Shoes were her one weakness, and she
indulged herself shamelessly, secure in the fact that
few people ever noticed.

Ben Frazer was the kind who noticed. "I
wouldn't be wearing Ferragamos when we traveled," she said. The moment the words left her
mouth she could have cursed. She'd already tacitly
accepted the fact they were going together.

If he recognized he'd won, he didn't show it.
"Good thing," he drawled. "We'll take off tomorrow morning, head south toward the lake region by way of Las Palmas. I know a few people
who might have some idea where your sister is,
and who she's with."

"She's with someone named Ramon. I think
he's a rebel of some sort."

"Big help, sugar. Do you know how many men
are named Ramon in this country? And the sides
in this little conflict seem about evenly divided,
and one person's rebel is another person's patriot.
Besides, what makes you think she's still with
him? Is your sister the type for long-term relationships?"

He already knew the answer, Maggie thought.
He just wanted to make her say it. "No."

"All right, then. We'll leave tomorrow morning for the capital. And don't look so distraught—I know a better route than the one the bus took you. You'll pack light, dress down and wear better shoes. You'll let me ask the questions and you'll stay meek and quiet."

There are no better shoes, she thought mutinously, but she said nothing. "And how much am I paying you for this little task?"

"All expenses for both of us. It's up to you if you want to pop for separate hotel rooms—I don't mind sharing. Ten grand if we find her, five grand if we don't."

"That's outrageous!" she protested.

"Haven't you figured out that I am outrageous? You don't have a whole lot of choice."

"Five thousand if we find her, two if we don't."

He leaned back. "You impress the hell out of me, Maggie. Nothing like haggling when your own family's lives are at stake."

"I'm a banker," she said sternly. "I take money seriously."

He hooted with laughter. "I should have known. Do you have a calculator for a brain and an adding machine for a heart?"

"I don't think you need to worry about my

heart, Mr. Frazer. It's not going to have anything to do with you."

His slow, lazy smile was quite possibly his most potent weapon. She wanted to slap it off his face, and yet at the same time it stirred odd, unexpected feelings in the pit of her stomach.

Hunger pangs. She hadn't eaten since morning, and then it had only been some limp toast. "I don't…" she began, when Señora Campos herself set down two big bowls in front of them. The stew was savory, rich-smelling, with beans and rice and chunks of meat, and she could only be glad her stomach never growled loudly.

"Señor Frazer ordered for the two of you, Miss Brown," she said. "This is our house specialty."

She'd been planning on ordering a plain grilled chicken breast. Maggie had never been one for spices, or ethnic food in general. Her father always used to say they were two of a kind. They liked food they could recognize.

She didn't even want to speculate where those chunks of meat came from. With Señora Campos beaming down on her, and Ben Frazer watching her with his mocking eyes, she had no choice but to pick up a fork and start eating.

The first bite made her cough and choke, and she reached for the first thing at hand. It turned out to be Ben's bottle of beer, but she was in no condition to quibble.

"Good, isn't it?" Ben said cheerfully. "Señora Campos prides herself on her cooking. Try another bite—it gets easier on the virgin palate."

She glared at him, about to inform him that nothing about her was virgin, when she thought better of it. With Señora Campos standing there she had no choice but to take another, smaller bite, bracing herself for the fiery heat of the spices.

Her eyes were watering, but she chewed gamely, fighting her way past the initial assault of the stew. It was surprisingly delicious.

"It's good," she said, forgetting to mask the surprise in her voice.

"You need a little spice in your life, sugar," Ben murmured lazily.

"I don't need anything in my life but my sister's whereabouts," she said, taking another drink from his beer. The stew was wonderful, but it had to be washed down with something cooling. "I'm very happy with my life."

"You have a man, Miss Brown?" Señora Campos asked.

If it had been Ben she would have dumped the stew in his lap. As it was, the kindly lady who ran the small inn meant well, and Maggie summoned up a faint smile. "Not at the moment, *señora*," she said.

Señora Campos cast a fond look at Ben, then back at Maggie, and a benevolent smile wreathed her face. *"Bueno,"* she said. "I'll bring more beer," and she disappeared back into the cantina.

Maggie had lost her appetite. "What did you tell her?"

"That you had hired me to help you find your sister. After all, she was the one who sent you to the bar in search of me. It's not my fault she's an incorrigible matchmaker. She's been trying to set me up for as long as I've been here. I'm a challenge to all the matchmakers in San Pablo and trust me, there are far too many of them. They never give up hope."

Her curiosity got the better of her. "And just how long have you been here, Mr. Frazer?"

"Long enough. You done hogging my beer?"

She hadn't realized she was still holding it. She handed it back to him, turning her attention to the stew. She was getting used to the fiery strength of it—her eyes barely watered anymore. They ate in silence, and she kept her eyes focused on the rapidly disappearing stew. She was going to have miserable heartburn that night, and if she had any sense she'd push the bowl away. But it was too tempting.

She looked up into his eyes. They were as tempting and dangerous as Señora Campos's fiery stew.

She set down her fork. "If we're leaving first thing tomorrow morning then I'd better say good night. I have a lot of things to do if I'm going to be ready."

"Such as?"

"Such as none of your business. What time do you want to leave?"

"First light. Have you got cash?"

"Travelers' checks. And an ATM card."

He snorted. "You really don't have any idea what you've gotten yourself into, do you?"

She pushed away from the table. She'd had enough of Ben Frazer for one day, and they hadn't even spent an hour together. Stella was going to owe her, big time for this. "But you're going to keep me safe, aren't you? That's what I'm paying for, isn't it?"

He smiled, his slow, devastatingly sexy smile. "Don't worry, Maggie. I'm going to take real good care of you. And that's a promise."

EL GALLITO HAD SEEN ENOUGH. The two bickering Americans weren't going to spend the night together, more's the pity. It would have made his life a lot easier, but in the end it was unimportant. There was nothing he was going to do about it until they led him to his eventual target, and in the meantime it didn't bother him if they wanted to sleep in different places or wanted to do it in the middle of Señora Campos's neat little patio.

He snorted, enjoying the image. She was a pretty little thing, a bit small and pale for his tastes, but she'd likely be terrified of him. He liked it when women were frightened. Maybe he'd forget about chivalry and do her before he killed her. And make Frazer watch.

He shrugged, pushing away from the doorway where he'd been planted, motionless, for the past few hours. He'd better keep his thoughts on his job, not on his pants. The Professor had proven almost impossible to kill. Holed up in some mountain hideout in the north of the country, he was waiting until the elections were finished. He thought he'd come down to the capital and take the reins of government from El *Generalissimo* with no arguments, just because he'd won the vote of the people.

And he would win, there seemed no doubt of that now. No matter how many people had been bribed, threatened, bullied or coerced, there were still enough left, along with the stinking UN observers, to ensure that the thirty-year government of Generalissimo Francisco Cabral was on its last days.

Unless something happened to his opposition. All it would take was a single bullet and the people would once again turn to Cabral as their savior. Sheep, that's what they were, and they needed to be guided by a strong, forceful hand. The *Generalissimo's* iron fist.

And El Gallito was his right hand man. He prospered under the current government, and he'd told the general that this particular job was free. His campaign contribution.

Because if Generalissimo Cabral's dictatorship toppled, then so would the comfortable life of El Gallito Loco.

And some things were just worth fighting for.

He didn't bother following Frazer through the damp night air. He already knew where he was staying, knew where the Jeep was. He'd put a tracking device behind the back seat, but he wasn't counting on that for the answers. He intended to stay within range of them as they led him straight to his quarry.

Frazer would leave at dawn, as he always did. The question was, which direction? Would he head south, to the lakes, north to the capital, or would he go west into the mountains. Word had it that Morales, The Professor, was hiding out in the mountains.

El Gallito hadn't thrived in the business of assassination without having developed impressive instincts, though. He was counting on Las Palmas. He'd be waiting for them, keeping his distance, and if Frazer didn't pass his hiding place by eight in the morning then he'd simply circle around and find out where he did go.

But he wasn't troubled by doubts. This was all going according to plan, and the woman would force him to take his time, making it all that much easier for El Gallito to follow them.

And in three days, by the time the results of the election were announced, The Professor and half his followers would be dead.

Including Ben Frazer and the American woman with the silly shoes.

And El Gallito Loco would be secure once more, ready to face a comfortable retirement.

CHAPTER THREE

"I SAID 'FIRST LIGHT.'" The voice came to her out of the darkness, and Maggie sat up, so fast she slammed her head into something solid, something that went "*ooof,*" something that hurt. Ben Frazer was leaning over her in the darkness of her tiny hotel room.

"What the hell are you doing here?" she demanded, yanking the covers up to her chin. "And how'd you get in—I know I locked the door."

"What I'm doing is trying to get out of here before too many people wake up and start asking questions, Maggie. And I picked the lock—I have all sorts of unexpected talents."

"Great," she muttered.

"Oh, trust me, you'll be happy to make use of some of my more nefarious skills if the occasion calls for it. Get up. I've got coffee and rolls in the Jeep."

"I'll meet you out there."

He still didn't move. He was wearing a different

shirt—this one was blue and had at least a few more buttons, and his long hair was wet, presumably from a shower. He hadn't bothered to shave. And he looked far too at home standing by her bed. "You can get up now—I promise I won't look."

"I'm not moving until you're out of here, and the longer you stay the longer it'll be before we leave."

The damned man sat down on the bed, and she had to scoot over rapidly so he wouldn't sit on her feet. "I think we better get a few things straight, sugar," he drawled.

"Don't call me sugar," she snapped.

"You don't happen to be particularly sweet," he said in a musing voice. "Maybe I like the irony of it."

"Maybe I can find someone else to help me."

"Ask Señora Campos. Without me you'd be squat out of luck. And that's what we better make clear. From now on I'm in charge. You do what I tell you, no questions asked, when I tell you. This country is a boiling cauldron, and I have no intention of getting burned. The only chance we have of finding out who has your sister and getting her safely out of here is if you do what I tell you."

"What do you mean, who has my sister? You think someone's holding her hostage?"

"There've been rumors," he said. "I told you, we have a lot of warring factions in this country. If she's in the lake region, it's in the heart of bandit territory."

"I didn't come prepared to pay ransom," Maggie said, worry superceding other issues, such as his body far too close to her legs.

"We're not going to pay ransom. We're going to get her out."

"And you can do that?"

He nodded. "I can do that. If you do exactly as I say."

It all seemed so simple. Do what the man said, and he'd find Stella and get her back. So why was she resisting?

"Okay," she said. "You're in charge."

"Good. Now get the hell out of bed." Before she even realized what he planned to do he'd risen, caught her shoulders and hauled her out from beneath the covers to stand on the bare wood floor.

Dead silence. "Well," he said in a bemused voice. Unfortunately he was so surprised he didn't realize his hands were still clamped on her shoulders, and she couldn't yank free and dive back beneath the covers.

It wasn't as if she expected anyone to actually see what she slept in. She was the soul of practicality as far as the world could tell, but even the most pragmatic of humans could have a fanciful streak, as long as they indulged it carefully.

Maggie was careful. She bought ridiculously extravagant shoes, which people seldom noticed. And erotic sleepwear, since she always slept alone.

The current outfit, brought along because it was easy to pack, was a leopard-patterned velour halter and matching thong panties, which exposed at least six inches of flesh between the bottom of the tank top and the top of the glorified G-string. All exposed to Frazer's unblinking gaze.

She was too mortified to even move. And then she jerked herself out of his grasp, grabbed the sheet off the bed and draped it around her body with all the dignity of a Roman goddess. "I'll be ready in five minutes," she said in an icy voice, daring him to say anything.

Ben Frazer was smarter than she'd given him credit for. He didn't say a word, simply backed away, his face expressionless. "The Jeep's parked out back. I'll be waiting."

The door closed behind him, and she still didn't move. She wasn't sure whether to be relieved or insulted. He'd done nothing but get on her nerves since they'd first met, and now when he had something real he could use to taunt her, he was unnaturally restrained.

She dropped the sheet, looking down at her body with a distant eye. It was a good body, good proportions, maybe a little thinner than she would have liked, a little less chest than she would have liked, but all in all she didn't have much cause for complaint.

So why hadn't Ben Frazer acted like a ravening wolf?

Relief, that was what she was feeling. Sheer relief. It was bad enough that he was obnoxious and offensive—at least he wouldn't be coming on to her as well.

She dressed quickly and efficiently, tossed the rest of her clothes into her carry-on and was out the door within the five-minute time period. She found him in the Jeep, feet propped up on the open door, his hat tilted over his eyes as if he had all the time in the world.

"I have to find Señora Campos. I haven't paid my bill yet."

He shoved his hat back, and in the early-morning light he looked like a bandit himself, with his scruffy face and long hair. What in the world was she thinking of, going off into the unknown with him?

"She knows we'll be back."

"We will?"

"It's a small country, Maggie. Once we get your sister we'll circle back here and settle your accounts before we get you out of San Pablo for good."

Considering that was exactly what she wanted, there was no reason she should have been annoyed with his plan. Of course he wanted her out of San Pablo. That's what he was being paid to do. But she couldn't keep a tiny bit of doubt and suspicion from dancing in her brain. Why was he so eager to get rid of her?

She didn't have much choice in the matter. He was still lounging there, looking at her, so she dumped her suitcase in the back seat of the Jeep and climbed in beside him. He ran his eyes down her efficient, travel-proof clothes. "Khaki's the wrong color for you, sugar," he drawled. "It washes you out."

"Thanks so much for that fashion tip. You said you had coffee?"

"In the thermos at your feet. There are sweet buns there as well. You look like you could stand to pack on a few pounds."

It was the final straw. "Forget it," she said, reaching for the door. "I'll find someone else—"

He caught her wrist as she tried to slide out of the Jeep, and she bit back a little yelp of pain. He was strong, very strong, a fact that both unnerved and reassured her. "I told you, there is no one else," he said mildly. "Drink the damned coffee and we'll get out of here."

"Then stop picking on me." Once the words were out she realized she sounded like an adolescent whose braids had been tugged.

"But you're so much fun to tease, Maggie," he said. He was still holding her wrist, his long dark fingers wrapped around her paler flesh, but it didn't hurt. "If you didn't rise to my bait each time I wouldn't be so tempted."

"Fight the temptation."

He didn't say a word, just looked at her. And then he released her wrist and started the Jeep, moving down the alleyway before she could make up her mind to jump out.

She broke the silence as they reached the end of the small village. "There's no seat belt."

"Nope."

"What if we have an accident?"

"We'll probably die," he said. "But I don't intend to have an accident." He swerved to avoid a group of chickens wandering in the road. He was driving fast, and besides lacking seat belts the open Jeep seemed to be lacking shocks as well. It was going to be a long day.

"You're such a careful driver?"

He turned to look at her, not at the road, as they barreled along. "No. But I'm damned good at surviving. Be grateful you ran into me and not some loser."

"Oh, I am," she said sweetly. "Every waking moment."

The coffee was sweet, strong and milky. She drank it out of the thermos since he'd taken the only cup, wincing as some splashed onto her chest. The buns were still warm from the oven, a fact that brought her her first moment of comfort in what seemed like centuries but in fact was only about a week since Delia had announced she was dying and sent Maggie to fulfill her deathbed wish. She was trapped in a miserable situation and the only way to survive was to count her blessings. Good coffee. Great buns. A plan to find her sister after nothing but dead ends. And Ben Frazer seemed to have lost interest in talking, a rare boon indeed.

"Maggie," he said, out of the blue, destroying that particular illusion. He drove too fast on the miserable, rutted dirt roads, but she didn't waste her time telling him to slow down. She knew a contrary man when she met one.

"Yes?" She kept her voice cool and unwelcoming. Maybe she could slide down in the seat and close her eyes, pretend to sleep. Except that she had to hold on to the torn seat with both hands to keep from being bounced right out of the vehicle.

"You don't seem like a Maggie to me. That's much too friendly and down-to-earth for a banker from…where'd you say you were from?"

"Philadelphia."

"Figures," he said. "I'm surprised you aren't Margaret. You look like a Margaret to me. Actually you look like a Harriet, but I don't suppose that's an option. Unless your middle name's Harriet."

"It's not."

"So who called you Maggie, Margaret? Someone with a sense of humor?"

"My name isn't Margaret."

"What is it? Magda?"

"If this is your idea of pleasant small talk I'm perfectly willing to do without it."

"You know why you can count on me to find your sister?"

"No."

"Because I'm tenacious. I never give up. What's your name?"

He was going to find out sooner or later. It was on her passport, her ATM card, which he'd already assured her was useless, even on the travelers' checks. "Blanche Magnolia," she said.

Her careful driver swerved, just missing a tree. "Blanche Magnolia? And your sister's name is Stella?"

"Stella Hyacinth, as a matter of fact. My mother was fond of Tennessee Williams and spring flowers."

"I see. Couldn't you get it legally changed?"

"I love my mother, Mr. Frazer."

"I love my mother, too, but not if she'd named me Hyacinth Magnolia."

"Blanche Magnolia. And if it were you you'd have a lot more to complain about."

He was back to watching the road, thank God, but he spared her a passing glance anyway. "Very funny, *Ms.* Magnolia," he murmured.

"There'll be a bonus in it for you if you don't call me that name. I'm offering cash incentives."

"Ah, but there are some pleasures that money can't buy," he said. "We should be in Las Palmas by dinnertime. I'm afraid we're not going to be in the best part of town."

"I've been to Las Palmas. I didn't even know there was a best part of town."

"Honey, if you stayed near the airport you were in the high-rent district. Las Palmas is a pit."

"Why?"

"Corruption, poverty, you name it. Generalissimo Cabral knows how to run a country efficiently. Keep the people too hungry and downtrodden to do anything but try to survive."

She looked at his cynical expression. "You sound like a revolutionary yourself, Frazer."

"Not me, Maggie. It ain't my country, and I'm not about to risk my neck for it."

"Then why are you here? What brought you to San Pablo in the first place?"

"You want to hear the story of my misspent life, Maggie? I'm flattered. I didn't think you gave a damn about me."

"I don't." She wouldn't look at his face, so she concentrated on his hands as he held the steering wheel, far too loosely given the state of the roads. He really had beautiful hands. Long, long fingers, narrow palms, no rings. For all she knew he was married. And why the hell would it matter if he was?

"Then why are you asking?"

"Forget it. It was brought on by a fit of boredom. How long will it take till we get to Las Palmas?''

''Depends on the condition of the road and how many times we're stopped.''

''Stopped? By whom?''

''Damn, I don't know if I've ever heard someone say 'whom' before in my life,'' he said in mock admiration. ''You sure know how to make a feller feel like a peasant.''

''Frazer, you are a peasant,'' she said. ''Who's going to stop us?''

''The national army, bandits, revolutionaries, any or all of them. Take your pick. You just keep your mouth shut and let me do the talking.''

''Lucky me.''

''Lucky you. I'll keep us out of trouble, I promise you that much.''

''I thought you promised me more. I thought you promised me my sister.''

''So I did, sugar. We'll find your sister no matter how long it takes.''

''I can't afford to have it take long. My mother's gravely ill. Not to mention the fact that I have a job. My plane is leaving Las Palmas in six days time. If we haven't found Stella by then I'm just going to have to go back without her.''

''You could always go back now. Return to your

poor mother's side, not to mention the bank, and when I find Stella I'll ship her home to you.''

"And I'm supposed to trust you to do this?" Maggie asked. "I don't think so. I wasn't born yesterday, Frazer. I'm not going to hand you a chunk of money and free rein. You're going to take me to find my sister."

"Suit yourself, sugar," he said, pressing down on the accelerator so that the Jeep bucked again. "In the meantime, you better prepare yourself. It might be wiser if we shared a hotel room. It's none too safe where I'm taking you."

"Then why don't we stay in a better place?"

"Because the pimps and the informers and assorted other bad guys don't hang out in the better places, Maggie," he said patiently.

"I'm sure I'll be perfectly fine. I'm used to traveling on my own all over the world."

"Ever been to a place like San Pablo? Because until you have, you don't know squat."

"I'll be perfectly fine," she said again, her voice getting testy.

"Chill, *señorita*. Just trying to be of service," he said. "Besides, you've got a good strong voice."

"What's that got to do with anything?"

"I'll just come when I hear your scream."

And he gave her a charming grin.

EL GALLITO HAD NO IDEA WHY Frazer was taking the American woman the most circuitous route he could find, but there was no doubt he was heading north toward Las Palmas. It had been easy enough to ask a few questions of the people who worked for Señora Campos, and he hadn't had to approach the old lady himself. Just as well. She reminded him of his grandmother, and he still harbored a superstitious fear of the old lady, decades after she'd died from a fit of bad temper.

It made life easier for him. No need to keep pace behind Frazer's Jeep, bouncing over some of the worst roads in San Pablo. He could take a short cut, wind up in Las Palmas hours ahead of time and be lying in wait by the time they showed up.

There was always the chance the woman would insist on heading to a better part of town, but El Gallito was putting his money on Frazer. He'd tuck the two of them somewhere in the Old Town, where he could keep an eye on her.

The question was, why had he gone north at all? The boy who worked at Señora Campos's had told him that Frazer had informed the girl they were heading south to the lake region, and the young man had taken one look into Gallito's eyes and wouldn't have dared to babble anything less than the truth.

But he'd gone north anyway, leaving him no choice but to follow.

There was no way The Professor was in Las Palmas—Cabral would have heard and made short work of him. The only reason the man had survived so long was that he was in hiding, out of reach of Cabral's military executioners and his handpicked goons. Out of reach of everyone except the best of the best. El Gallito Loco.

Ben Frazer was good, good enough to have survived encounters with him in the past. But he was also a creature of habit. Chances were he'd go straight to Elena Barasos's place for the night. If he didn't spend the night between the American woman's thighs then he'd head out to find a game, probably at Jaime's or Salazar's.

And from what he'd seen of Frazer and the woman, it didn't seem likely they were going to spend the night between the sheets. At least, not together.

It wouldn't take much to disguise himself. He'd be waiting at Jaime's, and if Frazer didn't show up he'd head on over to the Hungry Dog. Frazer wouldn't recognize him, and the girl wouldn't know enough to be careful. Maybe he could find the answer from her and go straight for the kill.

But life was seldom that simple for a hardworking man, El Gallito thought wearily. He was prepared to do it the hard way. For San Pablo.

For Cabral.

And mostly for himself.

CHAPTER FOUR

MISS BLANCHE MAGNOLIA BROWN was sound
asleep in the seat beside him, no mean feat considering the state of San Pablo roads and the lack
of shocks on his Jeep. She started out by faking it,
probably because she didn't want to have to talk
to him anymore, but eventually it slipped into real
sleep, and she curled up in the ratty front seat of
his disreputable vehicle, bouncing with every jolt.

Her hair was coming out of that tight-assed little
knot, curling around her forehead. And speaking
of tight-assed. He was still dazed by the sight of
her in that get-up she slept in. For once in his life
he'd been struck dumb, unable to come up with a
fast comment or a lewd remark, and damn, did that
woman deserve a lewd remark. Especially considering the way she reacted to the least little comment on his part.

But the sight of her standing there in that skimpy
sex kitten outfit had knocked him sideways with
emotions he couldn't even begin to sort through.

It wasn't as if he weren't damned well used to sex, to skimpy clothing, to any and all forms of titillation. Anyone else wearing that jungle outfit would have raised an appreciative physical response but nothing more.

But Maggie Brown hit him a lot harder than that. It was the contradiction. The touch-me-not coating of ice around her, the flinty eyes, the soft mouth, the way she had of meeting him toe-to-toe while part of her was shivering with some kind of reaction.

He couldn't figure her out. Was she cold as ice, or vulnerable in ways that were far too tempting? He shouldn't even be thinking about it.

He knew what he was going to do—it was much too important to get Miss Maggie Brown as far away from her missing sister as was physically possible. If he had to kidnap her, drug her, sleep with her, or dump her on the bandits' doorstep, he had to do what needed to be done to keep her from interfering. In the end she might forgive him.

Or maybe not.

It didn't really matter. Once everything was taken care of Miss Maggie Brown could throw any kind of hissy fit she wanted. He hit a particularly deep pothole, and she jolted awake for a brief moment, her rich brown eyes staring up at him dazedly. She closed them quickly, obviously not cheered by what she saw, and a moment later she was asleep again, or doing a good job of faking it.

She probably faked orgasms, too, he thought coolly. She probably did it with another banker, beneath the covers and in the dark of night, and thought that was all there was to life. He'd be more than happy to broaden her horizons, given half a chance.

She wasn't going to give him half a chance, though. Sure, she had a way of looking at him when she thought he didn't notice, but it wasn't particularly female admiration. It was more the fascinated expression of a quivering brown mouse confronted by a hungry boa constrictor.

Six days. Six days till she got on that plane back home. He could manage to kill six days on the road in San Pablo. Mind you, it was one hell of a small country, but the roads were so awful it made travel dangerous and endless, and after living here for more than five years he knew almost every back road and dirt track and goat path in the country. Even avoiding the mountains, he'd have enough to keep her occupied. Besides, she clearly had no idea what kind of situation she'd gotten herself into.

He should feel guilty, if not about Maggie then about her dying mother. And he did feel guilty—

there was just enough decency left in his worthless
hide to feel regret that the senior Mrs. Brown
wouldn't get to see Stella before she bit the bullet.

Then again, people had a habit of outliving
everyone's direst predictions. In the meantime, he
was in the unpleasant position of having to play
God, and he was making his choices. In the scheme
of things, one dying old lady didn't mean a hell of
a lot.

And one starched-up, neurotic young woman
didn't mean much, either. So he felt a passing
amount of lust for her. He'd have to be half-dead
not to react to that outfit she slept in.

But then, if he was honest, he'd lusted after her
from the moment she marched into Miguel's cantina with her suit and her high-heeled shoes. He'd
peered at her from under his hat and almost wanted
to crawl out the back door. He knew trouble when
he saw it, and she had his name written all over
her.

He could have bailed. Found someone else to
take his place. He'd been at loose ends, waiting for
the week-long elections to conclude, and he'd
jumped at the chance to do something other than
wait. Anyway, it had been his idea to come after
her in the first place. All he had to do was make
a few calls and someone else would be commis-

sioned to take her on a wild-goose chase and he could have been free.

He was a man who did his damnedest to avoid doing things he didn't want to do, and yet he had no intention of leaving Magnolia Brown to anyone else's tender mercies. Besides, he'd promised The Professor he'd take care of it. It was the least he could do.

"Are we ever going to stop?" Her plaintive voice took him by surprise. So she hadn't been asleep after all.

He glanced over at her. "Why?"

"I'll give you three guesses and the first two don't count," she shot back. "Besides, I'm starving."

He pulled off to the side of the road, no mean feat considering how narrow and rutted it was. "There you go, kid. And you thought I wasn't amenable."

"You don't want to know what I think of you," she muttered, glancing toward the copse of trees. He waited for her to ask about a town, a bathroom, but she simply climbed out of the Jeep and headed toward the trees.

He waited until she disappeared into the small grove, waited just long enough, and then called out, "Watch out for snakes."

He expected to see her back at the Jeep in a matter of moments, white-faced, breathless, her clothes hastily pulled together. To his surprise she emerged from the woods several minutes later, calmly strolling back to the Jeep as if she had all the time in the world.

"Nice try," she said when she reached him. "I had a pet snake when I was a child. They don't scare me."

"There are some sandwiches in the back if you're hungry," he said, climbing out of the Jeep. "Some bottled water as well."

"Where are you going?"

He grinned at her. "I'm not afraid of snakes, either."

THEY REACHED THE OUTSKIRTS of the capital city by nightfall, a neat trick considering it was only forty-three miles away from Las Cruces. The roads alone would have killed half the day, and his circuitous route took care of the rest of the time. He drove through the countryside around the city, planning to come in from the north for no other reason than to disorient her. Besides, the inn he had in mind was so disreputable he was pretty sure she'd refuse to go there if she thought there was any alternative. He didn't intend to give her any.

She was silent as they drove past the outskirts of the city, past the slums and the graffiti-bedecked buildings that were Generalissimo Cabral's idea of affordable housing. She didn't realize he was watching her, as her face grew still and her eyes grew wider.

He pulled up outside Elena's place. "I'll get you settled first before I go out looking for information. Whether you like it or not I think we'd better share a room. This isn't the safest part of town."

She glanced at the tumbled-down hotel. "Then why are we here?"

"I told you, informers don't hang out in the tourist sections. Besides, you've never experienced a country until you've seen where the real people live."

"I'm sure the ones who live in the mansions near the airport are just as real as these people are."

"They're part of the military government. More robot than human," he drawled, climbing out of the car and grabbing his suitcase. Deliberately making no effort to take hers. He wanted to see if she'd ask him to, or if she'd try to make it on her own.

She slid out the other side, grabbed her suitcase without hesitation and started after him. "I'm sure

I'll be just fine in my own room," she said calmly. "I have faith in the inherent goodness of people."

"Then you came to the wrong country. Poverty puts quite a dent in people's sense of hospitality."

"Nevertheless..."

"Nevertheless you'll do as I say. That's what you promised, before I took you off on this ridiculous journey."

"When it was a matter of safety, yes, but I don't think—"

"I'm not interested in what you think, Maggie. I doubt there's a single place that's safe in all of San Pablo right now, what with the elections, and the slums of its capital are probably the worst. You'll do as I say or I'll dump you here and let you fend for yourself."

"And what makes you think I can't do just that?"

"Because you don't speak the language and you don't have a gun. And because you may terrorize the bankers in Philadelphia but you aren't going to frighten a San Pablo pussycat. You're powerless here, sugar, and you need me. I thought you'd accepted that fact."

He didn't expect her to admit it, and she didn't. But she stopped arguing, following him into the dimly lit entrance of the hotel without a word.

"Frazer!" Elena flew from behind the desk, wrapping her sturdy arms around him and pressing him against her overflowing bosom. He kissed her soundly, making it a noisy one to annoy Maggie.

"We're looking for a room, love," he said.

"Of course you are, you bad boy. Where did you get the little nun? She's not your type."

Fortunately for Maggie's temper she spoke in her San Pablo Spanish.

"I'm democratic when it comes to women, sweetheart. I love 'em all."

"Of course you do. You want the honeymoon suite? Nice big bed and a view of the city."

"She doesn't need any view but me, *pequena*. Give me my usual room—that'll be good enough. And see if Luis can rustle up some dinner for her. I have to go out, but I think it's better if she stays behind. I don't want her too tired out for tonight," he said with a deliberate smirk.

Elena howled with laughter and swatted him on the arm. "If she is, you just come and find me. I don't tire so easily."

"I remember."

"What are you talking about?" Maggie said from beside him, that cranky, constipated expression on her face.

"Just talking about the weather, sugar."

"I thought you were supposed to be talking about my sister."

"All in good time. Elena and I are old friends. We have to observe the formalities."

"How old a friend is she? She looks younger than I am. And I certainly don't see anything formal between the two of you," she grumbled.

He turned to look at her, his eyes deliberately wide and innocent. "Why, sugar, you sound like you're jealous."

Elena let out a snort of laughter. She leaned closer to Maggie. "You got yourself a lot of man," she said in English. "You get tired of him, you just send him my way and I'll take care of him real nice."

"Behave yourself, Elena," he said. "Maggie will think you're serious."

"Have him," Maggie said. "Be my guest."

This was getting past amusing and heading over into dangerous. He took the risk of moving away from them, leaning over the desk to grab the key to his usual room.

"Why you want that room, Frazer?" Elena had switched back to Spanish. "That bed's too damned small to have any fun."

"Don't worry your pretty head about it, love. I'm very inventive." He looked back at Maggie, and an unexpected trace of regret washed over him. She looked exhausted, her skin pale, her brown eyes hollow, even her hair drooped. They hadn't had much to eat—just some sandwiches Señora Campos had packed for them, and the endless ride in the Jeep even left him feeling a little worn-out. It wouldn't have been so bad on paved roads, but he'd taken some of the worst roads, and in San Pablo you had to hold on to your seat to make sure you didn't go flying. Riding in a vehicle was far from a passive occupation.

"Come on, Maggie," he said, taking the suitcase from her. He was right—she was too tired to even protest. "We'll get you settled and then find something to eat."

"I'm not hungry."

"Well, you should be. And I'm starving. This way." He started toward the narrow stairs. Either she'd follow him or not. If she didn't, he'd wash his hands of her and someone else could take on the dubious task of distracting Magnolia Brown.

She was right behind him when he unlocked the door to his usual room. By the time he pulled the string and turned on the overhead light she was already in, and he moved fast enough to stop her from leaving once she caught sight of that sagging double bed.

She looked at him with a trace of her usual cool. "And where are you sleeping?" she asked pointedly.

"Maggie, you wound me," he protested. "If I wanted to force myself on you then I would have chosen someplace along the way, out of earshot."

"Maybe you prefer beds."

"Maybe I do," he said with a slow grin. "But I'm still more interested in keeping you out of harm's way than getting into your pants. This is my usual room when I'm here. It's got the best location—it looks over the back alley, it's near the stairs and it's a short drop to the ground if we have to leave through the window."

"Where are you going to sleep?"

"You really have a fixation about that, don't you, Mag?" he drawled. "I've slept on more than my share of floors in my lifetime, and this one's no better or worse than many of them. You can enjoy the sanctity of your virgin bed."

She sat down on the virgin bed, and for a brief moment her shoulders sagged. Then she sat up straight, not wanting to betray even a moment's weakness. "Good. I just hope you don't snore."

"I think my snoring will be the least of your worries," he drawled. "You look beat. I'll have Elena bring you up something to eat while I go out and see what I can learn. There's a local bar with just the sort of people I'm looking for.''

"I'm coming with you. It's my sister—''

"You're staying put. You'll keep the door locked and you'll scream good and loud if anyone tries to open it. Most people wouldn't think to mess with you once they know you're with me, but there are always the few, stupid exceptions.''

"They're all so afraid of you?'' she scoffed. "I can't imagine why.''

He smiled at her. His ferocious, wolflike smile that tended to terrify braver souls than Maggie Brown.

"Can't you?'' he murmured. She looked up at him, and he could see the first trickling of real uneasiness in her stern brown eyes.

"Lock the door behind me,'' he said. And he was gone before he could ruin the effect.

CHAPTER FIVE

MAGGIE SAT ON THE SAGGING bed, listening as his footsteps died away. And then she flopped backward onto the mattress, staring up at the ceiling, the lone lightbulb hanging in the center illuminating the shabby interior of the room. It seemed relatively clean. She didn't want to think about how recently the sheets had been changed.

At least she was alone. Without his eyes watching her, those enigmatic, electric-blue eyes of his.

She could hear her stomach rumble. She hadn't eaten much for lunch—the constant jolting of the Jeep along the barely passable roads hadn't done much for the state of her stomach. But now that the bouncing had finally stopped she was starving.

Frazer had said Elena would bring her something to eat. Probably laced with cyanide. If Elena and Frazer weren't something more than friends then she was a kangaroo. Why he bothered making her sleep in the same room when he had such a luscious armful available was beyond her comprehension. She didn't believe for one moment that it could be that dangerous in this tiny hotel. It wasn't any noisier than most cities, though the occasional shriek from the alley outside was slightly unnerving. He was probably exaggerating the danger in order to keep her compliant. As far as she could tell the most dangerous creature in the entire country of San Pablo was Ben Frazer. She'd seen no signs of any alleged bandits, revolutionaries, or even the snakes he'd promised.

Her stomach made a rumbling protest again, and she allowed herself a faint, self-pitying moan. She would have given anything to be back in Philadelphia, in her safe, comfortable bed. She would have given anything to have spent her entire life without making the acquaintance of Ben Frazer.

She should be used to it by now. Her sister and mother had gotten her into more hassles than she could even begin to count, and ever since her father's death all the responsibility for them had fallen on her own shoulders. Not that it was a heavy burden—she was used to taking care of things, of cleaning up after her sister's mistakes, of soothing her mother's melodramatic extremes. This was a little more strenuous than the usual, but chances were this wasn't the worst trial she was ever going to face.

She just wished she'd had a chance to call home again, just to make sure her mother was hanging in there. If Delia was as sick as she said she was, she might already be dead, with both of her daughters thousands and thousands of miles away. If she didn't bring Stella back in time she'd never forgive her sister. If she didn't get back in time she'd never forgive herself.

Maybe she could just fall asleep, listening to the steady murmuring of her empty stomach. There was nothing she could accomplish tonight—she'd promised Ben that she'd stay put. Even if she went out in search of a public telephone there was no guarantee that she'd find a working one. And there was always the remote possibility that he wasn't exaggerating the danger.

She heard the soft, furtive footsteps above the noise of the city outside, coming down the hallway to her room. She sat up, all thoughts of sleep vanishing. She hadn't gotten up to lock the door when Frazer had left her—she'd just lain on the bed and felt sorry for herself. Maybe if she moved really fast she could reach it in time to keep out whoever might be coming for her.

She was halfway off the bed when the door opened, illuminating Elena's voluptuous figure. She was carrying a tray, and from across the room

Maggie could smell the onions and tomatoes and peppers, and her stomach knotted in anticipation.

"Dinner," she announced in her strangely accented English. Maggie was educated enough in Spanish and French to get her through most difficult situations, but the language of San Pablo was mostly beyond her comprehension. Throughout its troubled history San Pablo had been isolated from its neighbors but not immune from their influence. It was a strange combination of Spanish, French, Andorran and Basque traditions, and the language was a sort of mishmash. Every now and then she could pick out a word or two, but mostly it was as incomprehensible as ancient Egyptian.

Elena set the tray down on the rickety-looking table, then took the seat opposite, clearly waiting for Maggie to join her. She'd brought some sort of savory stew, accompanied by a cold bottle of beer, and any thoughts Maggie had of resisting vanished.

She was halfway through the stew when she looked up to meet Elena's dark, curious eyes. "It's very good," she said lamely.

"And you were very hungry. That's not like Frazer—he usually takes better care of his women."

"I'm not one of his women," Maggie protested. "I just met him."

Elena laughed, a throaty, sensual sound. "He had me on my back in less than an hour, *señorita*."

"I wouldn't be bragging on that if I were you," Maggie replied stiffly.

Elena laughed again, unoffended. "You're much too civilized. Here in San Pablo life is simple. You take love where you find it, because who knows when it will come again."

"Love?"

Elena shook her head with mock pity. "All women love Frazer. And he loves them in return, with all the generosity of his heart."

"Trust me on this, he doesn't love me. He doesn't even like me."

Elena frowned. "Impossible. Frazer likes all women. He flirts as naturally as he breathes."

"He doesn't like me," Maggie insisted. "And the feeling's mutual. Thank God. I will admit I've done nothing particularly likable as far as he's concerned. I'm sure he gets along beautifully with most other women."

Elena stared at her. "This is serious," she said grimly.

"Hardly. I don't expect everyone to like me." Actually that wasn't true. Maggie did her absolute best to be pleasant and agreeable to almost everyone she met. Ben Frazer was one of the few exceptions. He got under her skin like a poison ivy rash, but she wasn't about to explain that to Elena.

"You don't understand. Are you trying to tell me that Frazer hasn't tried to seduce you?"

"Apart from a few rude comments, no."

"And has he put his hands on you?"

"No, to that as well. He'd be sorry if he did."

"Frazer isn't the kind of man who worries about such things," Elena said, deep in thought. "Drink your beer."

"I'd better not. I'm a cheap drunk."

Elena looked at her curiously. "What does that mean?"

"It means that it takes about one beer to affect my good judgment. Two beers and I'm swinging from the chandeliers and singing torch songs. I find it much safer not to drink at all."

"If you wanted a safe life you shouldn't have come to San Pablo, *señorita*."

"Didn't Frazer tell you? I'm looking for my sister. He was hoping he'd find some lead—"

"He didn't say anything about your sister. He said you were a rich tourist out for a little excitement and he was going to provide it for you. I promise you, he can be very exciting."

Maggie reached for the beer. It was strong and skunky and delicious, and she swallowed a good

third of it. He hadn't even asked Elena if she'd
seen a tall, redheaded beauty. Damn the man!
"Where did he go?" she demanded.

"The Hungry Dog. It's a bar down the
street...where do you think you're going?"

Maggie had already risen. She took another deep
swig of the beer. Dutch courage, she thought. Or
San Pablo courage. "I'm going to go find him and
remind him why he brought me here."

Elena raised her eyebrows. "I thought you said
you weren't involved with him. He won't like being dragged back here, even for sex."

"I'm not interested in sex or in dragging him
back here!" Maggie protested. "I want him to do
his job so I can get back home." She started toward the door, but Elena was faster, blocking the
way.

"You're not going anywhere, *señorita*," Elena
said. "I promised Frazer I would keep an eye on
you and that's exactly what I intend to do."

"Fine. Keep an eye on me. I don't mind the
company." She tried to dart around her, but Elena
shifted quickly, still blocking her way.

"I'm bigger than you are, *señorita*," she
warned.

Maggie didn't even blink. "Yeah, but I'm fast

and determined. You can come with me or get out of my way—those are your two choices.''

Elena glared at her. And then a slow, rich laugh burbled out of her throat. "Does Frazer have any idea what he's gotten himself into with you?"

"If he doesn't he's about to find out."

"This I must see. All right, little one. We'll go find your lost man and you can give him a piece of your mind. Want to finish your beer first?"

She took it and drained it, looked at the empty bottle and then sighed. "I'd sell my soul for a Diet Coke," she said mournfully.

"That's about the going rate in San Pablo for such luxuries. Have you changed your mind?"

"Follow me," Maggie said recklessly, starting toward the door.

A broad grin lit Elena's face. "No, *niña*. This is my neighborhood. If you want to find Frazer, you follow *me*.''

FRAZER LEANED BACK IN HIS chair, peering through the cloud of smoke. The pile of winnings at his elbow was substantial, but he hadn't come to the Hungry Dog to play poker with the cream of the San Pablo underworld. He'd come for information, and so far he'd gotten nada.

He couldn't rid himself of the feeling that someone was watching him. Following him. It made no sense—he wasn't the one in any potential danger. As far as he knew, no one connected him with Stella Brown's lover, any more than they knew what possible use Maggie might be. There was no reason to think anyone might be watching him.

The whiskey was watered down, the cards were marked and Carlos Salazar was a cagey old bastard who wasn't telling him a damned thing he didn't already know. Ben Frazer wasn't in a good mood.

"What do you think of the elections, my friend?" Carlos asked lazily, squinting at his cards through eyes made bleary with too much smoke and whiskey. "You think Morales stands a chance against the *Generalissimo?*"

"If the good general doesn't manage to have him killed first," Frazer said calmly.

"He hasn't managed it yet. You'd think with the thousands of soldiers at his command he'd have more success in ending one troublesome life, but no. He's even made overtures to some…acquaintances of mine, to see if they were willing to take on the job." Salazar squinted his bleary eyes in the semblance of a smile.

"And did your friend take the job?"

Salazar grinned his particularly ugly grin. "I told him not to."

"That surprises me. The *Generalissimo* has always been oblivious to some of the more unconventional dealings of this area. I would imagine The Professor would be a lot more interfering in some of your activities."

Salazar shrugged. "Call me a foolish old sentimentalist," he said. "Perhaps I love my country even more than I love my income. The Professor might be a welcome change from the *Generalissimo*."

"Perhaps," Frazer murmured, unconvinced.

"And what's this I hear about the little American you have stashed over at Elena's place? Why are you here with old men like me, rather than warming her bed?"

Frazer grinned. "Women can wait. You don't think I'm at her beck and call, do you?"

"If you think women can wait then you've never been married, my friend," Salazar said sagely. "I hear she's looking for her sister. A tall redhead."

Frazer shouldn't have been surprised that Salazar knew his business. News always traveled fast in San Pablo. He shrugged. "We don't spend much time talking."

Salazar laughed. "You're too good a poker

player, Frazer. You don't give anything away. So what about her sister?"

"I'm sleeping with her, not the sister."

"I should hope so. Or The Professor might have your huevos for lunch."

Frazer picked up the hand that Salazar had just dealt him. Three jacks and two losers. Salazar wouldn't want to lose that substantial pile of money in the middle of the scarred table.

"I don't think so." He pushed the two smaller cards toward the dealer, one of Salazar's silent compatriots. "I'll take two."

He heard the noise from a distance, the sound of breaking glass, the voices raised in warning. And above it, Elena's rich laugh. What the hell was Elena doing here? She'd promised to watch over Maggie and make sure she didn't get into trouble.

He didn't move, though it took all his concentration to keep utterly still as he took the two cards that were dealt him. He was about to turn them over when the door to the back room opened, revealing his worst nightmare. Maggie Brown, in a righteously pissed-off mood.

The room froze into silence with her approach, and Frazer leaned back in the chair lazily, watching her. Knowing that everyone was a fascinated witness to this confrontation.

"What the hell do you think you're doing?" she demanded, coming up to him. She looked tousled, softened a bit despite her rage. Her hair had come loose, and it was a tangle of waves around her face. Her khaki shirt was unbuttoned an extra button, revealing a surprisingly generous cleavage that was doubtless accentuated by her deep, furious breathing.

"Playing cards," he said lazily, reaching for the two he'd been dealt. He put them in his hand, controlling his groan of dismay. A full house was all well and good, but he really wasn't thrilled to have drawn two queens. A red one for Stella, a black one for Maggie. And she was looking positively black-hearted with rage.

Still, it was a good enough hand to win the pot, and he pushed his substantial winnings toward the center of the table, ignoring her.

Big mistake. She stalked up to the edge of the table, caught it and dumped it before anyone could stop her, tumbling the cards and the money into a hopeless jumble on the floor.

He heard Elena's hiss of horror as he saw all three of Salazar's men draw their guns. He almost dove in front of her, a strangely quixotic urge, when Salazar spoke.

"Basta!" he said. "Let's see how Americans discipline their women."

Oh, crap, he thought. Now they probably expected him to backhand her across the face to prove his manliness.

"Hell, we don't discipline our women," he drawled, not moving from his chair. "We cower in fear."

"You son of a bitch!" Maggie snarled at him. "You haven't even asked—"

It was time for him to make his move. He rose, caught Maggie by the shoulders and hauled her up against him, planting his mouth down on hers and silencing her in a time-honored tradition.

He could hear the shouts of approval from Salazar and his men. He could hear Elena's snort of laughter. He could taste the beer and spices of Maggie Brown's soft mouth.

And then he stopped thinking altogether, when she kissed him back.

CHAPTER SIX

TROUBLE, HE THOUGHT, nothing but trouble, as he wrapped his arms around her body, pulling her closer. Her arms were around his neck, and he wasn't quite sure how they got there when she'd looked as if she wanted to kill him, but there was no question that she was kissing him back. That she'd opened her mouth for him, that it was her tongue touching his and he was suddenly, instantly randy, so much so that he would have swept the winnings off the table and dumped her there himself if it had been available.

But she'd already done that, he realized, as reality began to intrude. And a moment later he felt her body tense, and before he could move her foot came down hard on his at the same moment she shoved him away.

She was wearing her damned high heels, and even through his heavy boots it hurt like hell. He cursed, fluently, and Salazar laughed.

"Your woman doesn't know how to respect

you, Frazer," he said cheerfully. "But since she managed to destroy our little game I'm sure you'll agree that the winnings are mine. I would have won that last hand anyway. I had three kings."

Frazer wasn't about to argue when he could do no more than growl. That had been a nice piece of change, and unlike his little banker-companion he didn't have enough money to throw away.

Maggie was standing there, breathing deeply, her rigid body daring him to strike her. He'd never hit a woman in his life, at least not since kindergarten when Betsy Morton had punched his best friend, but at that moment he was as strongly tempted as he'd ever been. "Where's my sister?" she demanded in a strangled voice.

"You're looking for your sister, *señorita?*" Salazar broke in, before he could silence her again. "Well, why didn't Frazer mention that? I'm the man who knows about such things. Carlos Salazar, at your service."

Maggie turned her stony gaze to Salazar, and Frazer wondered if she'd underestimate the plump, genial-looking old man smiling at her. Salazar would feed his own mother to the dogs for money. If he even knew who his mother was.

Maggie fell for it hook, line and sinker. "Do you have any idea where my sister might be, Señor

Salazar? Frazer promised to help me find her, but then he disappeared and I didn't feel like waiting.''

"You must learn patience, little one," Salazar said with a wheezy laugh. "Frazer would have gotten around to finding out what he doesn't know, sooner or later."

Salazar's choice of words had been deliberate, and Frazer tensed, wondering if there was any way he could interfere.

"I've heard there's a tall, redheaded American woman in the western district, up in the mountains," Salazar said, casting a mischievous glance at Ben's stoic expression. "You'll find her there, I expect. Frazer knows the route."

She cast a bitter look at him. "He told me he heard she was in the southern region."

"By the lakes? No, *señorita*. But then, that's why Frazer has come here, is it not? To find out exactly where your sister is? He knows where to find the truth, even if it takes him a while to get to it."

"*Gracias*, Salazar," Ben said in a gritty voice.

Salazar's beaming smile was malicious. "I am always eager to help my old friend. And such a lovely woman as well."

Ben reached over to take her arm. "Let's get out of here," he said.

As he'd half expected, she tried to jerk free, but he wasn't about to release her. Salazar was enjoying himself, but he was still as deadly as a cobra, and Frazer needed to get her safely out of there. And then start convincing her that her sister, Stella, was nowhere near the mountainous western provinces.

"I don't want to go anywhere with you," she said in a furious voice, but he ignored her, dragging her toward the door.

"Go with Frazer, *señorita*," Salazar said. "He'll be able to find your sister better than anyone. And Frazer…"

"What?" He didn't bother disguising his furious snarl.

"You might keep your eye out for El Gallito Loco. Word has it he has an interest in The Professor."

Damn Salazar. That was what he'd been trying to find out, and Salazar had known all along. He halted, still holding Maggie's elbow in a tight grip. "You think so? He's an old man—I thought he'd retired."

Salazar grinned in the dim light, exposing his impressive false teeth. "I know so, old friend. And he's ten years younger than I am. In the prime of life. Still more than a match for you."

"Why didn't you try to stop him?"

"What can I say? I brokered the deal."

Frazer's response was pungent and obscene, enough that even the unflappable Elena drew in a shocked hiss of breath, but Salazar just laughed, unmoved.

"Don't worry, Frazer," he said in his rich, San Pablo Spanish. "I just like to even up the odds a little bit. It makes things more interesting. Enjoy your pretty little one tonight. Her anger should make it even better."

"If she doesn't stab me in the throat," Frazer said gloomily. He was back in possession of his emotions. Salazar knew he'd gotten to him with the mention of El Gallito, but that was all he planned to give up.

"Do her once for me, old friend. If I were ten years younger she wouldn't be leaving this room with you."

"If you were ten years younger I'd ram those shiny new teeth down your throat," Ben said coolly.

Salazar chuckled. "Feeling possessive, are you? I don't blame you. She's a pretty little thing."

"She's a pain in the butt. I had no intention of taking her into the mountains."

"Of course you didn't. I find it much more interesting this way. Besides, I gave you El Gallito. Surely that's worth something."

Maggie tried to yank her arm free, but he wasn't about to release her. "What are you talking about?" she demanded in English.

"Come along, *niña*," Elena said. "You really wouldn't want to know."

Since she couldn't very well go without him, and Salazar had said all he was going to say, Frazer simply nodded, heading out the door with the two women, one hostile, one amused.

Maggie was wise enough to keep quiet until they got out into the alleyway. "What did he say to you, you lying son of a—"

"Watch your mouth, Maggie," he drawled. The word hung between them, loaded. He'd done more than watch her mouth. And she'd responded, to his everlasting shock.

"Wait till we get back to the hotel, *niña*," Elena murmured. "You never know who might be listening."

It was dark enough in the alleyway that Frazer didn't have to conceal his surprise. Elena was one of the shrewdest, toughest women he knew, and she didn't have much use for the rest of her gender. And yet she was surprisingly solicitous of his pain-in-the-butt companion. Not like Elena at all.

He waited until they were inside the small lobby of Elena's hotel. "What the hell did you mean, bringing her there?" he demanded in his fluent San Pablo dialect.

"Speak English, Frazer," Elena admonished him in that language. "It's rude to hold a conversation that other people can't understand."

He was not only fluent in San Pablo Spanish but adept at swear words, and he let loose with a torrent that would have made a sailor blush. Elena only smiled. "Behave yourself," she said sternly. "The *niña* would have gone out alone looking for you, and heaven knows what kind of trouble she would have gotten herself into. It was lucky I decided to look after the poor baby."

"She's probably older than you," he growled, lapsing into English.

"Only in years, Frazer. She's as innocent as a babe when it comes to men like you."

"You may as well speak in Spanish if you're not going to include me in the conversation," Maggie broke in, clearly irritated.

"Go up to bed," Frazer growled.

"Not until you answer some questions. Who's El Gallito? And why were we heading south when my sister is in the mountains?"

"That's what Salazar says. What makes you

think he's to be trusted?'' Frazer countered, annoyed. He'd hoped she'd missed the reference to El Gallito.

"What makes you think I'd trust you?" she snapped.

"Because you were fool enough to come with me. If you don't trust me then why the hell did you hire me?"

"Because I didn't have any choice. Now I do. I imagine Señor Salazar could find someone to help me—"

"You know what Salazar said when we left?" he asked her in a silky voice. "He told me to do you one time for him. And that if he were ten years younger you wouldn't have left the room. He wasn't talking about choice, either, sugar. You go back there and he's not going to give a damn about those ten years."

She looked shocked, and he muttered another, obscure curse word. Elena was right—she was an absolute infant in the ways of San Pablo. If he wasn't there watching out for her she might disappear into one of Salazar's cribs and never be heard from again.

He didn't like to think what The Professor would say to that. He didn't like to think how he'd feel about it himself, either. He didn't like her, that much was sure. She was prissy and annoying and inconvenient, and the last thing he wanted to do was play nursemaid.

Of course, the first thing he wanted to do was take her up to that bed, strip off her clothes and spend the rest of the night helping her grow up. The fact that he wasn't going to touch her again wasn't helping his thoroughly bad mood.

"Go up to bed, Maggie," he said again, weary now. "If we want to get a decent start you'll need to get some sleep."

"Where are you going to sleep?"

"Are you offering to share the bed?" He didn't bother waiting for her outraged denial. "I'll be sleeping on the floor. Don't worry—I've slept in worse places."

"I'm not worried. I just don't want any unexpected visitors."

He allowed himself a slow, lazy grin, one that effectively terrified most men. She blinked at him, uncertain what to think. "They won't get past me. Tomorrow we'll head south…"

"West," she said. "Salazar said she was in the west, in the mountains."

"And you believe him?"

"Isn't that why we came here? Why you were

with him? To find out where Stella is? Well, he told us."

"He certainly did," Frazer said in a grim voice. "We'll head into the mountains. Fair warning, though—the roads aren't nearly as good as the ones we traveled on today."

"Those were good roads?"

"San Pablo's finest highways," he lied. "Go to sleep, Maggie. I promise not to wake you when I come in."

She sure as hell didn't like that idea, though he wasn't sure what was bothering her. Whether it was going up there alone or the knowledge that he was going to be joining her.

She had nothing to fear from him. He wasn't going to touch her again, no matter how tempting. He glanced over at Elena, wondering whether she might be interested in a little distraction for old time's sake. He doubted it.

He looked at Maggie's cute little butt disappearing up the stairs. It was going to be a long, hard night.

In more ways than one.

THE MAN SLIPPED OUT of the crowded bar, humming softly under his breath. He owed Salazar a debt for this one, though Salazar had no idea he'd been there in the shadows, watching, listening. No one had thought to look closely at the old man drinking whiskey and smoking cigarettes, no one had wondered how he'd gotten in there.

Part of his stock in trade. He could wander in anywhere, and no one would notice. Not even Salazar, who had half a dozen armed guards watching over him at every moment.

He could have succeeded where a dozen others had failed, killed Salazar and been gone before anyone realized what happened. But he had no reason to kill him. Not unless someone paid him. El Gallito Loco didn't waste his talents for free.

Still, he'd warned Frazer, and El Gallito could have done without that. Not that Frazer was any match for him. Maybe once, long ago, he'd gotten the better of him. Or, to be completely accurate, twice. But it wouldn't happen again. El Gallito was on his guard, and Frazer was distracted by the girl.

They were heading up into the mountains, and somewhere in that rough terrain was the headquarters of Ramon Morales de Lorca y Antonio, known affectionately as The Professor because of his studious looks and learned manner. And if Frazer thought he wasn't going to end up taking the girl there, then El Gallito would set him straight.

Two days before the elections were done with,

two days to finish with The Professor and ensure the *Generalissimo's* future. And his own.

It could be done. It would be done. Or El Gallito would die trying.

MAGGIE OPENED HER EYES slowly, the heat of the room pressing down around her. It was still dark, the bed was a hollowed-out nest beneath her and she wasn't alone.

She stretched out a hand, very tentative, but there was no one on the right side of the bed. She moved her foot to the left, but still nothing.

And then she realized that her head was about to explode.

The moan that slid from her throat was unconscious and heartfelt. It wasn't fair! She'd had one single bottle of beer and she had a merciless hangover. Her mouth tasted like cotton, her head pounded and she felt as if she'd been dragged along the ragged length of San Pablo. Which, in fact, she had.

A disembodied voice floated out of the darkness. "You can't be feeling that bad. Elena said you only had one beer and you got to sleep in the bed. I had too much whiskey and a mattress on the floor and I'm feeling quite chipper."

Maggie rolled over onto her stomach and

moaned into the pillow. "Do you have to be so damned perky?" she groaned. "I wake up slowly."

"Perky's my middle name. And you don't have the luxury of lying around, bright eyes. We'd better get the hell out of here before Salazar decides he's not too old for you."

He'd come to stand by the bed, looming over her, but she wasn't about to look at him. "I need a shower," she muttered into the pillow.

"And I need a shave. We'll both have to do without. You nearly blew it last night, but I'm too noble to abandon you as you deserve. Up and at 'em, Magnolia."

"Don't call me that." She rolled over on her back to glare at him. Big mistake. He was shirtless, sleepy-looking, unshaven and oddly, unsettlingly tempting. She couldn't still be drunk, could she? Not on one beer.

"Out of bed, Maggie, or I'll drag you out myself. I want to see if you're wearing that tiger-striped outfit again."

"It was leopard. And I threw it out."

"Tell me you're lying, angel! That outfit's gonna haunt my dreams."

All right, so he wasn't going to go away. She

sat up. "We're heading west." It wasn't a question.

And he wasn't about to argue. "We're heading west," he said, clearly resigned. "But it won't be my fault if we end up on a wild-goose chase. Salazar's the last man to trust—he's head of the San Pablo crime world. He doesn't do anything unless there's something in it for him."

"Who better to get information from?" He wasn't going to move, Maggie decided, and she was foolish to hesitate. After all she was wearing boxers and a T-shirt—more than enough to cover anything of interest to him. Ignoring him, she threw back the covers and got out of bed.

"Maybe the man you hired to be your guide?" Frazer countered. He was looking at her, letting his eyes run over her as she stood there.

"Maybe I'm having second thoughts."

He didn't move. "Say the word, sugar. I've got better things to do than haul your ass around San Pablo while you bitch at me. Yes or no, Magnolia Brown."

He was standing too close to her in the dark, hot room, though in fact he hadn't moved. There was no reason to think he was asking for anything more than her trust. No reason to think she was committing to anything more.

But she was. And it frightened her. All she had to do was tell him no, ask Elena to find her a taxi to the airport and she'd be back in the U.S. by nightfall. For all she knew Delia had gone from bad to worse, and she needed at least one of her children with her at the end. Even though she almost certainly would have preferred it to be Stella, her flighty soul mate, and not the dull, dutiful daughter.

Leave, her mind told her. Get the hell out of this country, away from this man. This man who, oh my God, kissed her last night, she remembered suddenly. No sweet little kiss, either—it had been a scorcher.

It must have been sheer surprise and instinct that had made her kiss him back. That and the effect of the beer.

No, she couldn't blame the beer for that. It had been his mouth. His undeniably luscious mouth.

"So what is it? Yes or no?"

It took her a moment to gather her distracted thoughts. She took a step back, away from him, and the smothering heat of the room vanished, leaving her chilled. No, she thought. No way, not ever.

"Yes," she said.

He was completely unimpressed. "Then get your butt in gear. I'll be in the Jeep."

The door slammed shut behind him. "'I'll be in the Jeep,'" she muttered in a sarcastic tone. "What the hell am I, your faithful dog?"

She started after him, almost falling over the bedding on the floor. He'd dragged a mattress in to sleep on, and she hadn't even heard him. What if he'd been Salazar?

Not that she believed for one moment that she had anything to fear from that sweet old man. Frazer was just trying to scare her.

Still, better the devil you know than the devil you don't know. And she had little doubt that Ben Frazer was a devil indeed.

CHAPTER SEVEN

IT WAS A FULL HALF HOUR later when Maggie sauntered out to the alleyway behind the old inn. She'd found a lukewarm shower but no such thing as a hair dryer, and while it was still wet her hair lay flat and docile. Five minutes in the Jeep and she was going to look like a gorgon. Not that it mattered. Her only hope was that she'd scare Ben Frazer.

He wasn't a man who scared easily. The look he gave her as she climbed into the Jeep was so intimidating that a lesser woman might have quailed. But Maggie had made up her mind. She was putting her trust in Ben Frazer's hard, dangerous hands. She wasn't going to let him scare her as well.

"I said five minutes," he growled.

"I said I needed a shower," she responded with a false sweetness.

"You're wearing that?"

She glanced down at the simple dress she'd pulled on. "Obviously. What's wrong with it?"

"Per your orders, we're heading into the mountains. People don't wear skirts in the mountains."

"Tell that to the grandmothers of San Pablo."

"You sure as hell don't look like anybody's grandmother," he grumbled.

Before she could respond Elena appeared from the back of the hotel. The sun had just risen, but Elena looked more than half asleep.

She said something to Ben, but Maggie couldn't make out a single bit of meaning in the torrent of rich, rolling words. Whatever she said, Frazer didn't like it, and even if she couldn't understand his response she recognized his sentiment.

"As for you, *niña*, you keep him in line," Elena said to her in English. "He's a good man, but a bad little boy. He's met his match in you, I think."

"He has not!" Maggie said in horror.

Elena didn't argue; she simply shoved a package into her hands. It was hard, cold, wrapped in rags. "A present for you, *señorita*," she said.

"Back off, Elena," Frazer grumbled. "We're already late due to her ladyship's vanity."

"Maybe she wanted to be pretty for you?" Elena suggested.

Ben and Maggie protested in unison, but Elena

merely smiled wisely. "Go with God," she said. "Find the little one's troublesome sister, and watch out for El Gallito."

Frazer groaned something in Spanish, but this time Maggie understood at least enough of it. "Shut up about El Gallito," he growled, putting the Jeep into gear.

Elena said nothing, but when Maggie turned to wave goodbye she saw a faintly worried expression on the young woman's face.

"Just how well do you know Elena?" she asked, turning around and automatically searching for a seat belt before she remembered that Frazer didn't seem to believe in them.

"In the biblical sense," he said.

"I wasn't asking for details. Do you trust her?"

"With my life. Why? What did she give you? A bomb?"

Maggie looked down at the bundle in her lap. "Maybe a charm to protect me from people like you."

"Elena's not into witchcraft. She's too pragmatic. And in case you haven't figured it out yet, she thinks we make a cute couple."

"Oh, God!" she said in horror.

"My sentiments exactly," he drawled. "What's in the package?"

She unwrapped it gingerly, then let out a sound of awed delight.

Frazer jerked his head to look at her, but he couldn't see what lay in her lap. "What was that orgasmic sound?"

He was trying to embarrass her, but she was too happy to let him get on her nerves this time. "Don't be crude, Frazer," she said calmly. "That's not a sound you're ever going to hear from me." She unwrapped her treasure. "It's a cold can of Diet Coke," she said reverently.

He was looking at her as if she'd lost her mind. Which doubtless he probably believed. It wasn't her problem. The can was icy cold against her fingers, and the anticipation was heavenly.

After a moment of respectful silence she popped the top and drank half of it down, closing her eyes in utter bliss.

She knew he was looking at her. "Watch the road," she said, not bothering to open her eyes.

"Elena found that for you?" he said in a troubled voice.

She opened her eyes reluctantly. They were already past the outskirts of town, heading into the dawn-lit day. "She did."

"Hmmmph," he said. "She must really like you."

"Hard to believe, isn't it?" Maggie said, too blissed-out over the can of soda to take offense. "Not everyone finds me so unbearable."

"Not everyone finds me so unbearable, either," he drawled.

"Maybe you behave better around other people," she shot back.

"I doubt it. What you see is pretty much what you get. I just don't happen to rub people the wrong way. The way I do with you."

The vision of Ben Frazer, shirtless, hot, gorgeous, rubbing her any way at all was momentarily distracting. Disturbingly so. She made a noncommittal sound, taking another drink. She was right, the wind had already pulled her hair free of the tie. She was going to end up looking like heaven only knew what. Not that it mattered, of course.

"Diet Coke," Frazer said in a musing voice. "I don't remember the last time I tasted real live pop."

"I'm not about to refresh your memory," Maggie said. "If you want Diet Coke you can go back home."

"How do you know where back home is?"

"I assume it's somewhere in the United States. You must have family…"

"Not much family left, sugar. Just a brother out

in Los Angeles and a sister in college in Colorado. In case you can't tell, I'm not really the Southern California type."

She glanced at him. "No, you seem more like the Idaho survivalist type."

She'd surprised a laugh out of him. "Not that, either, but it's closer. I like wandering the world. There are too many interesting places to see, too many people to meet to tie myself down in one place. Maybe eventually I'll go back. And you're right, I'll probably pick someplace at the back end of beyond, though I have to admit politics aren't of much interest to me."

"Not even here? They're in the midst of a revolution, and you don't care?" she countered, shocked.

He shrugged. "Most leaders are the same, no matter what party they come from."

She glanced back at the huge storage buildings they'd just passed. There were huge faces plastered all over them, of a man in a uniform, his face pitted either with acne scars or the crumbling facade of the walls. The esteemed dictator of San Pablo. "So you support Generalissimo Cabral?"

Frazer shrugged again. "Why shouldn't I? Just because the U.S. doesn't like him..."

"He's a murdering fascist dictator," Maggie

said in shock. "How can you see the results of his government and not care?"

"And what makes you an expert on San Pablo all of a sudden? What would a banker from Philadelphia know about conditions in San Pablo?"

"I watch *60 Minutes*," she said.

He laughed. "Don't believe everything you see on TV, darlin'."

"Who's running against him in the election? Why isn't his picture plastered all over the place as well?"

"Because Cabral's the man in power, and he intends to keep the power by any means possible," Frazer replied. "And if you want to know what The Professor looks like, there's a newspaper under the seat. It's a couple of weeks old but I imagine his picture is in it."

She dragged it out. As usual, the *Generalissimo's* ugly face was plastered over the front page. The text, without the complication of the San Pablo accent, was slightly more discernible, and it was easy to pick up the flattering essence of the article.

"The Professor?" she echoed, opening the brittle, yellowing pages.

"Ramon Morales de Lorca y Antonio. Better known to the people of San Pablo as The Professor, who's fighting a losing battle against the General."

She found him on an inside page. He wasn't much more attractive than the ugly dictator, with a long, sorrowful looking face, a receding hairline, narrow stooped shoulders and glasses. He looked like a professor, all right. A scholar who lived in the intellect, not in the world. What good would he be against a military bully like Cabral?

"So you're on the General's side?" she questioned in disbelief.

"I didn't say that. I just like to win."

The Diet Coke was gone, the can empty and Maggie felt a fleeting pang of regret. She banished it sternly. "You're not the man I thought you were, Frazer," she said.

"Considering you've made it clear you think I'm the scum of the earth, I guess I should be gratified. I stick my neck out for no one."

There was something oddly familiar about that statement, and the way he said it, but try as she could to place it, it eluded her. And then she remembered. It was a line from *Casablanca*. But was Ben Frazer playing a part, or did he really mean it?

"So what if we find Stella among The Professor's followers?"

"Do you think that's likely?"

"No," she said honestly. "She goes for swashbucklers like you, not scholarly types. I can't see someone like The Professor exciting her romantic instincts."

"Swashbuckler?" he echoed, horrified.

His reaction was almost as good as the can of soda had been.

"She's too idealistic to be swayed by Cabral and his goons," she said. "But she might be with one of The Professor's followers. What would you do then?"

"Hand you over, take your money and get the hell out of there," he said. "Swashbuckler," he muttered again in disgust. "I am not a swashbuckler."

"We'll need to get back to Las Palmas. That was part of the deal."

He sighed. "Okay, I bundle you and your sister back into this Jeep, tie up your sister if she resists, fight off The Professor's men single-handedly and then get the two of you back out of the mountains and onto the next plane to the U.S. Simple. I think my price has just gone up."

They'd left the city limits and were heading toward the mountains looming in the distance. Maggie took one last look at The Professor's aesthetic countenance, oddly taken. He looked like a good man, unlike the fascist bully who ran the country. She shoved the paper back under the seat, grabbing onto the split leather seat as Ben ran over a bump in the road.

"How long will it take us to get into the mountains?" she asked.

"Most of the day. We'll head toward Segundo tonight. I have a friend or two in the area who might have some idea where Stella might be."

"Then why didn't we head there in the first place?"

"Because I'm still convinced your sister is in the southern lake region," he snapped.

She knew a moment's hesitation. Was she being crazy to insist he take her west? Was he taking her farther and farther away from her sister, when time was in such short supply?

The silence stretched between them as they moved deeper into the countryside, and when she finally broke it her voice wasn't as strong as she would have liked. "I need to find her, Ben," she said. "I need to trust you. We'll go where you say."

He didn't slow the Jeep, didn't even look at her, but she knew he was considering his options. Apart from that, she didn't have the faintest idea what was going on behind his tanned, impassive face, his electric-blue eyes.

"We'll head west," he said finally. "Salazar usually knows what he's talking about. Maybe we'll get lucky."

She allowed herself a cautious sigh of relief. She'd done it. She'd put her fate in his hands. Now all she had to do was really believe she could trust him.

She slid down in the seat, clutching the cracked leather with her fingers as they went over another bump. Even though the sun had risen the day was cloudy, hot and overcast, and ominous clouds hovered near the peaks of the mountains. "Does this vehicle have any kind of roof?" she asked.

"Nope. You afraid of a little rain?"

She sighed. "Swashbuckler," she muttered again, knowing it annoyed him.

The Jeep jerked ahead slightly on the bumpy road. "Cut it out," he growled, "or I'll feed you to the crocodiles."

"You have crocodiles in the mountains of San Pablo?"

"I'll import some."

She leaned back, satisfied that she'd annoyed him. It gave her a certain measure of security, knowing she got on his nerves. Elena said women adored him, and she could almost begin to guess why. There was no denying he was absolutely gorgeous, or would be if he had a shave and a haircut and a decent suit. And she'd seen flashes of his devastating charm—if he decided to turn that on a woman, then that woman would be hard put to resist. Even one who found him as totally obnoxious as she did.

A shave and a three-piece suit. She couldn't imagine it, didn't particularly want to. For some reason she didn't want to see him tamed and civilized like some...banker. And if she were completely honest with herself, she'd have to admit that it wasn't because she'd find him more attractive like that. If he were dressed like a banker, he'd be safe. And deep in her heart she didn't want him safe.

"Why did you kiss me last night?" She hadn't even known she was going to ask the question. It had been driving her nuts ever since she remembered, and she could still feel the damp heat of his mouth against hers, the rough thoroughness with which he'd taken her kiss. It might be the jolting of the Jeep, but she suspected it was something else causing her stomach to tighten into knots.

If she'd expected to surprise him by bringing up the subject she'd failed. He didn't even spare her a glance. "Why did I kiss you? Simple enough. You stormed into Salazar's place like a nagging wife, and it was the best thing I could think of to shut you up and to assert my authority."

"Your authority?" she echoed, her hands curling into fists.

"A woman without a man in a place like Salazar's is someone who's fair game. I had to claim ownership, and fast. I could have hit you, I suppose, but I figured kissing you would bother you more."

"Thanks," she said dryly. "I would have preferred the slap."

"I know you would," he said in a soft, treacherous voice. "So why don't you tell me why you kissed me back?"

THAT SHUT HER UP, as he knew it would. She slid down in the seat, arms folded across her chest, doing her best to ignore him. A good thing, too. She was getting to him better than anyone had in years, and it was taking far too much of his energy to ignore her.

It would be just as easy to wander through the mountains of San Pablo as it was in the lower altitudes, and up here they were less likely to run into people who could speak English and answer her damned questions. With luck they could be within a thousand yards of The Professor and his followers without her having a clue.

Besides, the moment he'd heard about El Gallito Loco he knew he'd had no choice. The Professor had to be warned. If he had to drag Maggie into the mountains, so be it.

She was getting harder and harder to distract from her goal. Or maybe that was because he was finding her equally distracting. He could smell the soap on her skin, the shampoo in her hair as it blew dry in the breeze. He could smell temptation and sin on the air. But he couldn't smell redemption.

There was only one way to shut her up, make her forget about her sister, her questions, her hostility. One way to turn her from a terrier with a bone to a soft, melting mass of femininity. He could take her to bed. And he didn't doubt for one minute she'd let him do it, against her better judgment.

Somewhere out there El Gallito Loco was gunning for The Professor. And if history could be trusted, he'd be gunning for Frazer as well. It was three years ago that he'd made his second attempt at killing The Professor, and Frazer had been there to stop him. He should have killed him then and there, but Frazer had a sentimental aversion to killing people. It certainly would have made things easier if he weren't hamstrung by scruples.

But then, if he weren't, he'd belong in the *Generalissimo's* camp.

He didn't know whether those scruples would keep him from taking Miss Blanche Magnolia Brown to bed.

He sure as hell hoped not. He was looking for an excuse, any excuse, to touch that mouth again. If it could serve to distract her from her incredibly ill-timed quest then it was a sacrifice he was more than willing to make, he thought with a wry smile. She'd told him he'd never coax that orgasmic sound from her.

He was going to prove her wrong.

EL GALLITO WAS HUMMING underneath his breath. Frazer's rusted out Jeep made so much noise that his quieter, modern SUV was drowned out. As long as he stayed out of sight he could keep pace with the two of them as they led him straight to his prey.

He hadn't expected it to be quite so easy. He didn't mind that Salazar had warned Frazer about him—it only made Frazer more determined to get to The Professor and warn him. He wouldn't linger in the mountain villages with his American girl-friend—he'd go straight to the source.

With luck, the job might be finished by nightfall, and El Gallito would be back in the capital in time to celebrate the election results. San Pablo law was very clear on such matters—if the elected official dies before he takes office, his opponent wins the position. Even if the people of San Pablo mourned the tragic passing of Morales The Professor, they would soon happily return to the old order of business under Generalissimo Cabral's firm rule.

In the meantime, El Gallito was content to enjoy the warm afternoon, the sunshine beating down in his late-model SUV, and hum beneath his breath. Any job worth doing was worth doing well.

And El Gallito Loco, the assassin, was a master at his craft.

CHAPTER EIGHT

MAGGIE LOOKED UP at the clouds overhead. The day had gone from sullen to threatening as they climbed higher and higher into the mountains, and Maggie's mood had gone from dire to deeply depressed. They hadn't passed a village, a farm, even a wild animal in hours, and Maggie couldn't rid herself of the fear that she'd made a very big mistake in insisting they head west.

Why had she thought that old man was any more trustworthy than Frazer? For all she knew he'd sent the two of them into an ambush. Didn't Frazer say he was some kingpin in the San Pablo underworld? He could be in league with bandits. There was a thriving trade all over the world in holding Americans for ransom, and she couldn't remember if she'd told anyone other than Frazer that she worked for a bank. Maybe they were heading straight into some bandits' lair, they'd cut Frazer's throat, hold her for some ridiculous sum of money her bank would refuse to pay, they'd rape and kill her and dump her body on top of Frazer's and no one would ever know what happened to her...

"What the hell's wrong with you?" Frazer demanded. "You look like a snake crawled up your leg."

She gave herself a little shake. "I told you I'm not afraid of snakes. At least, the non-human kind. And I'm tired. My imagination was running away with me."

"*Hmmph.* I like your orgasmic sounds better."

She ignored that. "You know what you're doing, don't you? I didn't force you to come this way when it's really dangerous?"

"Maggie, I hate to break this to you, but you'd be hard put to force me to do anything I didn't damn well want to do," he said lazily. "Break into that basket in the back and find me something to eat, would you? I'm starved."

"We aren't stopping for lunch?"

"We can stop, but any lunch we get we brought with us, so we might as well keep going."

"What about dinner?"

He grinned at her. "That's obviously your problem. I have fed you enough. Dinner depends on how far we get. There aren't any hotels or restaurants around here, babe. If we're lucky we'll make it to Segundo by nightfall, and we might be able to buy something there. Otherwise it's leftovers and camping rations. You'd be surprised how good freeze-dried chili can taste.''

''I'd prefer not to find out,'' she said, reaching behind her, holding onto the back of the seat as the Jeep continued its bumpy climb along the narrow roadway. The left side of the road hugged the mountain. The right side was a sheer drop-off into a rocky valley. Maggie had never been overly fond of heights.

She slid back into the seat, dragging the basket into her lap. ''Cheese, fresh bread, some fruit,'' she said, once she was settled. ''And a jar of something to drink.''

''Probably water,'' he said in disgust. ''Anything else?''

''If you're thinking I'm going to let you drink beer while we drive…''

''I was hoping for coffee. Lacking caffeine, I guess you're going to have to provide stimulation, sweetheart. Tell me the story of your life.''

''Yeah, right. Trust me, you'd nod off in seconds.''

He had a really devastating smile, Maggie thought gloomily. She'd really be much better off concentrating on the mountainous terrain and the hunk of bread she was chewing. Except that the steep drop-off was making her dizzy, and even Frazer's annoying presence was a welcome distraction.

"Humor me, Maggie. We've got a long way to go."

"I've already told you, I'm a banker from Philadelphia. A very good banker, actually. I'm vice president of my branch, and I have a talent for managing money."

"Does that mean you're rich? Maybe I should become a fortune hunter and seduce you."

"Fat chance," she scoffed. "And no, I'm not rich. I'm so busy taking care of other people's money that I don't have much time to see to my own. I live in a town house in Chestnut Hill, my mother lives in Merion, I live a quiet life."

"You live alone?"

"Yes."

"No boyfriend? Lover? Ex-husband?"

"None of your damned business."

"Too busy taking care of other people's money again? Or do you scare them off with your sweet demeanor?"

"You're the only one I'd like to scare off."

"You're doing a piss poor job of it, angel. Tell me about your family."

"There's not much to tell. Nuclear family," she

said shortly. "Born and raised in Philadelphia, with a responsible father and a flaky mother and sister. We took care of them, my father and I. Now that my father's dead it's up to me to see that they're safe."

He was silent for a long moment. "How old are you?"

"Twenty-eight."

"And how old is Stella?"

"I told you, we're twins. She's twenty-eight as well."

"And your mother?"

"Fifty-three. My father was a lot older than she was."

"So what makes you think you're responsible for a twenty-eight-year-old and a fifty-three-year-old? They're adults. They can look after themselves."

"You don't have any family, do you?" she countered.

"I have too damned much family. A brother in L.A., a sister in Fort Collins, aunts and uncles and cousins all over the place. The Frazer's are a damnably tight-knit group. It doesn't mean they can't look after themselves."

"Well, my family can't."

"Of course not. Not if they're used to counting on you to take care of them."

"Thank you, Dr. Freud," she said stiffly. "Shut up and drive."

"You're going to have to face it sooner or later, Maggie. You'd be much better off putting all that phenomenal energy into yourself. Your family will do just fine without you, hard as it is for you to admit it."

She opened her mouth to reply when the glowering sky finally decided to let loose. Within seconds they were soaked. She quickly shoved the loaf of bread back into the basket and covered it with the cloth, but water was already pooling in her lap and on the floor of the Jeep, and her clothes were soaked through to her skin.

Frazer seemed oblivious. The rain ran down his face in sheets, his eyes were narrowed against the blinding water, but he simply kept driving, intent on the roadway that was rapidly turning to mud.

"Aren't you going to stop?" she shouted over the noise of the downpour.

"And do what?" he shouted back. "There's no shelter around here. Might as well keep driving." The Jeep slid in the mud, moving sideways, and Maggie let out a strangled shriek. The road was steep and narrow, and nothing stood in the way of the sheer cliff.

She must have spent more miserable hours, but she was hard-put to remember. The rain didn't let up, the road, if anything, grew steeper and more narrow, and the mud turned into a soupy consistency as Frazer drove doggedly onward. Maggie clutched the seat in desperate hands, but the rainwater made the old leather slippery, and she kept losing her grip. She didn't bother complaining or screaming at Frazer, much as she wanted to. All she could do was close her eyes, try to hold on and pray.

They stopped so abruptly that Maggie was thrown forward, banging her forehead against the windshield. She opened her eyes, putting her hand to her face, only to bring it away covered with rain and blood.

She turned to look at Frazer, a dazed expression on her face, but if she expected concern she was optimistic. He'd already climbed out of the Jeep and grabbed his duffel bag and tossed it on the rain-soaked ground. She started to get out of the Jeep as well when he stopped her.

"You might want to stay put for the moment, Maggie," he drawled, kneeling on the front seat and looming over her. "It's a sheer drop on the other side."

She jerked her head around to look, and let out a quiet moan of sheer terror. They weren't hanging over the edge, but close enough that she might have slipped.

He was cupping her face, moving her hair away from her forehead. "Just a bump and a small cut," he said briskly. "These head injuries bleed like crazy. Hold on." He reached into his pocket and pulled out a handkerchief. She didn't move while he proceeded to tie it around her forehead like a bandage. "Climb out this way."

She didn't need to be told a second time. She scrambled out of the Jeep after him, landing on her knees in the mud, almost ready to kiss the ground in her relief. He hauled her upright with impartial concern, staring down at her bloody, rain-drenched face, and a small smile curved his mouth. His damnably sexy mouth.

"Now you're the one who looks like a swashbuckler," he said.

She yanked her shirt free and tried to wipe some of the blood away with the tail of it. He watched the process with annoying fascination, and she realized she was exposing most of her stomach in the process. She yanked the shirt back down, glaring at him.

"What are we going to do now?" she demanded.

"Looks like we're going to walk."

"Walk?" she echoed in horror. "In this rain?"

"The Jeep wasn't doing much good. Anyway, it's good and stuck."

"I'm not walking," she said. The sultry heat of the San Pablo lowlands had turned sharply colder in the mountains, and the rain seemed to have sunk to her very bones.

"Suit yourself," he said, tossing his duffel back onto the muddy ground. "I'm not carrying you."

He started up the muddy track that had once been a road, abandoning both her and the Jeep without a backward glance.

"You can't leave me here!" she cried.

He stopped and turned. "Then get your butt in gear and come with me. Or you can wait until someone shows up, though I hate to think who might be out in this kind of weather."

"What about your Jeep?"

"I'll get it later. It's just about out of gas anyway—we were going to have to start walking sooner or later."

Blanche Magnolia Brown, Philadelphia banker,

used a word she'd never used out loud before in her entire life. And then, for good measure, she kicked the Jeep.

She heard the groaning sound from a distance. And then she saw that the Jeep was moving, slowly, sliding backward toward the edge of the cliff.

She didn't even stop to think. She started after it, grabbing for the side in a ridiculous attempt to stop its momentum. In a daze she heard Frazer's shout of fury, and a moment later she was slammed full face into the mud, with Frazer's body covering hers.

A moment later he rolled off her, and she lifted her head to watch as the Jeep disappeared over the side of the cliff.

The noise it made as it tumbled down the hillside was endless, and she winced, hoping it would stop. But it didn't—on and on, as the noise grew fainter, the clang of metal against rock, of trees breaking.

She turned to look at Ben. He was lying on his back in the rain, breathing deeply, not even blinking as water splashed over his face.

Finally the noise stopped. "It didn't explode," she said in a small voice.

"Not enough gas left in the tank." His voice was calm, remote. He still didn't move.

She sat up. "I'm...I'm sorry," she said.

He nodded. And then he surged to his feet, effortlessly. He looked down at her. "You coming?" he inquired.

She nodded. She stood up, glancing over the hillside to the path of devastation. The Jeep was nowhere to be seen, but its trail had carved a swathe across the valley. "My suitcase," she said in a mournful voice. "My Ferragamos."

"Gone," he said grimly, unmoved. He looked at her. "Did you have any more of that underwear?"

"Yes."

"Damn." He picked up his duffel bag. "Come on, Maggie. You need to rescue your sister, remember?"

"I remember," she said. So the shoes were gone. And her ridiculously fanciful underwear. And her travelers checks and passport and ATM card and all her clothes. She had a kerchief around her head, she was soaked to the bone, and she'd just pushed a car over a cliff in a fit of pique.

She started to laugh. She threw back her head and laughed, in the face of the rain and the San

Pablo mountains, she laughed, the sound ringing out over the valley.

"Have you lost your mind, Maggie?" Ben demanded warily.

"No," she said, controlling her amusement. "I've lost everything else under the sun, and you're doing your best to take away my very reason for being here, but no, I haven't lost my mind. I just found my sense of the absurd."

She didn't expect him to get it. But a slow smile curved across his face, and he shoved his wet hair back, nodding with approval. "Maybe there's some hope for you after all, Miss Magnolia."

And for some reason she smiled back at him, no longer furious. "Maybe there is."

THEY'D GIVEN HIM A BAD moment there. When El Gallito had seen the Jeep tumbling end over end down the mountainside he'd thought his entire trip had been for nothing. If they'd crashed in the Jeep there would be no one to lead him to The Professor, and these mountains guarded their secrets too well. There was no way he could find his target in the next twenty-four hours without divine intervention, and El Gallito had learned that the Almighty didn't have a whole lot of sympathy for a hired killer.

But there'd been no screams, no death cry, no bodies flying from the open cockpit of the Jeep. And he knew Frazer far too well to expect him to make that kind of mistake. No, he and the woman were out of the Jeep before it made its abrupt descent, and Frazer had probably pushed it himself. He knew El Gallito was out for The Professor's blood—he was smart enough to assume he was being followed.

Not too smart if he thought he'd fool El Gallito with such a crude bluff. They were heading onward on foot, and they'd be just as easy to track. They'd be moving slower, and it wouldn't be long before he'd catch up to them.

He had to be very careful, though, and pick the right moment. When Frazer's defenses were down. He was a formidable opponent, and El Gallito couldn't count on the presence of the woman to effectively distract him.

He had a few hours to play with. It was growing late, they'd be wet and miserable while he was still safe and dry inside his sturdy SUV. When he was ready, they'd be defenseless.

He could hardly wait.

CHAPTER NINE

MAGGIE WAS SHIVERING. Her head hurt, though less than she would have expected, given her brush with the windshield on the erstwhile Jeep. She was soaked to the bone, and while the last downpour had the dubious benefit of sluicing most of the mud and blood off her, it left her chilled and achy and ready to weep with exhaustion.

She didn't say a word. She kept pace behind Frazer, moving steadily, and if she slipped on the wet pathway she simply got up again without a word.

It was getting dark. The road had turned into a narrow track, climbing higher and higher into the mountainous terrain, and she had no idea whether the altitude was getting to her or simply the lack of food and warmth. He was right—Stella could take care of herself in the future. And Maggie would tell her just that, if she ever managed to catch her breath long enough to speak.

She'd long ago lost any reluctant admiration for

Frazer's tall, strong body. He just kept moving, inexorably, and if there was a sort of catlike grace to him she didn't give a damn. All she wanted was a fire and a place to lie down and the world to leave her alone. Her amusement had fled long ago, and right now misery was her only companion. Frazer seemed to have forgotten about her entirely.

It was growing dark. The rain was still falling, a steady drizzle that kept Maggie's clothes drenched and her shoes squelching in the mud. She wondered what would happen if she simply sat down and refused to take another step.

Except that she knew what would happen. Ben would give her one last mocking look and abandon her, and it wouldn't matter at all that she'd asked him to bring her up here, paid him to do it.

And so she kept on, counting the steps as she went, so blindly wretched that she could barely speak. It didn't matter—there wasn't much to say. Sooner or later she'd simply drop in her tracks and that would be the end of it. No one would ever find her body, and she'd become a family mystery. Stella's grandchildren would always wonder what happened to their great-aunt Maggie, who disappeared in the mountains of San Pablo looking for...

What the hell was she looking for? Did she even care anymore? Could she walk one more step?

A tree branch slapped her in the face, and she had her answer. She went down, and this time she stayed down, sitting in the middle of the rocky path, trying to catch her breath.

She'd underestimated him. As soon as he realized she'd fallen behind he came back, looming over her in the gathering dusk. "We're almost there, Maggie," he said gruffly.

"Almost where?" Or at least that was what she'd tried to say. Her breath was wheezing, her words barely discernible.

"The place where we're stopping for the night."

She shook her head. "I'm...stopping here..." she gasped.

She wasn't expecting sympathy, or patience, which was a good thing because those two commodities were clearly in very short supply. She also wasn't expecting him to haul her straight up, into his arms.

"Put me down!" she said, struggling.

"If you don't hold still I'll send you after my long-lost Jeep," he said grimly. An empty threat— they were nowhere near the cliffs anymore. "There's a ruined farmhouse somewhere up ahead where we can find shelter. It's too far to Segundo tonight, and the accommodations wouldn't be much better. I'm tired and I'm hungry and I'm in one hell of a bad mood, so don't push me. Lie still and be quiet."

He'd started back up the steep pathway, seemingly unaffected by her solid one hundred and twenty three pounds in his arms. He was still carrying the duffel bag, and she knew that was a fairly hefty proposition as well. He didn't seem the slightest bit fazed by it. He was much stronger than she realized, much stronger than his lean, sinewy body suggested. She opened her mouth to voice one more protest, then shut it instead. What was that saying? Wisdom was the better part of valor?

Being carried was a lot less comfortable than it looked in the movies, she thought dismally. When Richard Gere swooped someone up in his arms it looked divinely romantic. When Ben Frazer swooped her up in his arms to carry her up a steep, rocky pathway it was jarring and uncomfortable, his grip on her was as impersonal as a baggage handler's, and each step made her teeth rattle.

She didn't say a word.

It was full dark by the time he set her down, and she was past noticing anything more than the basics. They were in some kind of shelter, and the rain had stopped. She curled up where he placed her, huddled and miserable, beyond words. She watched him as he built a fire in a pit in the center of the room, content to simply doze, when he finally spoke to her.

"Do you want to change first or eat?"

She roused herself. "Change into what? All my clothes went over the cliff with the Jeep."

"Mine didn't. You're caked with mud, sugar. There's a stream out back where you can wash off—it's not that cold. You'll feel better if you do."

"I doubt it."

"I can wash you myself."

She glared at him. It was probably an empty threat—he had to be almost as exhausted as she was, though he still appeared to be brimming with energy. It took all her effort to rise to her feet, but he wisely made no attempt to help her. "All right. Where's the stream?"

"Out back. I'll take care of dinner while you're gone."

"How domestic," she said with a trace of her usual fire, taking the pile of clothes he handed her.

The stream was easy enough to find—she just followed the sound of gurgling water. There was even a shallow pool, and it wasn't as icy as she'd feared.

They'd stopped at the ruins of an old farmhouse. Ben had chosen the one room that was reasonably intact, although most of the roof was gone. He'd built the fire in the middle of the floor, the smoke going straight out into the starry night. The rain clouds had finally cleared, and the night was still and beautiful. On any other occasion Maggie would have been awestruck by the sheer physical beauty of it. Right now all she could worry about was getting clean and dry.

The pool was marginally warmer than the running stream, and as quickly as she could she stripped off her muddy, rain-soaked clothes and jumped in. The water came to her thighs, and she sank down, shivering, rubbing the dirt away from her skin briskly. She even dunked her head under the water to wash away the stray blood from her forehead. The cut above her eye stung, but she was past caring.

No towel, of course. No underwear, either, though she could have hardly expected that Ben would come equipped with panties and a bra. Her own were too wet and muddy to even consider wearing, so she simply yanked on the baggy jeans, then grabbed the soft khaki shirt.

One button. One damned button and no bra underneath. He must have another T-shirt somewhere, but he hadn't bothered to give it to her, the pig. She had no choice but to tie the long tails of the shirt together and hope the one button would preserve what tiny amount of modesty she had left.

He was busy by the fire when she came back, and he didn't even bother looking up at her as she took a seat as far away from him as she could, on the other side of the blissfully blazing pit. Heat was wafting out of it, reaching into her icy bones, and her icy mood was beginning to melt as well.

She made one last effort to hold onto it. "Don't you have any shirts with buttons on them?"

He looked up, across the flames, and his innocent smile looked saturnine. "Not for you, sugar."

"Pig," she said without any real antipathy.

"You make a real nice swashbuckler yourself, Maggie," he drawled. "Or a pirate wench. How's your head feel?"

"Could be worse."

He came around the fire to her, so quickly she didn't have time to scamper out of the way. He caught her chin in his hand, pushing her wet hair away from her forehead with an impersonal touch. "It doesn't look too bad. Might leave a scar though. If you want I could try to stitch it."

She shuddered, and it had nothing to do with his hard, warm hand holding her chin, his cool, dark eyes staring down at her. "I thought you told me you couldn't sew."

"I save my tailoring talents for field dressings."

"I'll pass, thank you. Every good swashbuckler needs a scar or two."

An odd expression flitted across his face. In another man she might have called it tenderness, but Ben Frazer didn't have a tender bone in his body. He was still cupping her chin, and a strange silence had fallen between them, broken only by the sound of the crackling fire. He bent closer, and she had the craziest notion that he was going to kiss her, that he was going to put his firm sexy mouth against hers for no other reason than that he wanted to. And she wanted him to. Badly.

She panicked. She slid away from him, backward until she came up against the old stone wall of the room. "What's for dinner?" she asked breathlessly.

His eyes were opaque, giving nothing away, and she wondered if she'd imagined that strange, erotically charged moment. She must have.

"Freeze-dried beef Stroganoff," he said mildly. "Since you rejected the notion of chili. Washed down by whiskey."

"I don't think so."

"The whiskey's optional, though you've still got

a chill," he observed with clinical detachment. "The Stroganoff is an order. If you want to keep going you'll need to get a decent night's sleep and some food in your belly. Otherwise you'll probably collapse on the path again and this time I won't haul your ass anywhere."

"Charming," she said sweetly. She must have imagined that moment. "I'll eat."

"You'll sleep better with a couple of shots of whiskey as well."

"I'd sleep better in a nice warm hotel room on a real mattress."

"Wouldn't we both? Just be grateful I grabbed my duffel. We have two blankets between us. You can wrap yourself in one and hope for the best. Or we can team up and share them."

She didn't even dignify that with a response. The whiskey was sounding better and better. The idea of curling up on the hard ground with nothing but a thin blanket was about as appetizing as the tin plate of hot mush he handed her, but she didn't have much choice in the matter. Besides, it tasted surprisingly good. Maybe she'd sleep better than she expected. She was certainly tired enough.

The room was so small he could lean against the far wall and still be near enough to enjoy the heat of the fire. A little too close to her, but she was getting used to that. He'd eaten his dinner with methodical concentration, like someone taking medicine, and then he'd washed it down with some of the contents of a small, battered flask.

"You sure you don't want any?" He held it up in offering.

"I'm sure." She was leaning against the opposite wall. A little too far away from the fire for ultimate comfort, but a little too close to Frazer for her peace of mind. He'd managed to wash up as well, and in the flickering firelight he looked both beautiful and dangerous. Why in heaven's name had she ever gone off with him? She knew he was trouble the moment she laid eyes on him.

She must have been out of her mind.

FRAZER KNEW SHE'D BE trouble the moment he laid eyes on her. He had to have been out of his mind to continue with this little expedition.

If he'd thought clearly he could have dumped her anywhere along the way. Left her with Elena while he took off to warn The Professor.

Not that she would have been safe. Salazar had already known of her existence, and it had only been his own dubious protection that had kept her safe. If he abandoned her she would have been considered fair game.

Not that there was any reason he should feel responsible. She had chosen to come to San Pablo. She'd walked right into the lion's den with a singular disregard of the current political situation, and it would serve her right if she met with disaster.

He had too damned much conscience, that was his problem. He couldn't abandon a woman in those circumstances, not any woman. It didn't matter whether she was an American or not, or Stella's sister. It didn't matter that she brought out a crazy, protective, irritated streak in him that most people never came close to. He'd do the same for anyone.

So now that they were up here, less than a mile from the hidden valley where The Professor and his followers had set up headquarters, how the hell was he going to ditch her long enough to get a warning to them?

He could get her drunk, though she didn't seem terribly interested. He could try to sneak out while she was asleep, and if he didn't get back before she woke up he'd give her some embarrassing biological excuse that she couldn't very well question.

Or he could simplify matters, tie and gag her and simply go. It would keep her safe and out of the way, and while she'd be mad as hell when he came back, this whole wild-goose chase would be close to being finished. The elections would be over. Morales would be the newly elected democratic president, the *Generalissimo* would have no choice but to get the hell out of the country, and there'd no longer be any need to keep Maggie from finding out just what happened to her sister, Stella.

The one thing he wasn't going to do was sleep with her.

It was tempting, of course. He'd lain on the mattress last night, listening to the soft sound of her breathing, and it had taken all his considerable willpower to keep still. He could still taste her mouth, feel the heat of her skin. She was sitting there, looking half-dead, his clothes enveloping her, and if he had any excuse in the world he'd take her, here and now, and make her forget about her responsibilities and her sister and her bank and her life in Philadelphia.

How in the hell could he want someone who chose to live in Philadelphia? He was a wanderer, a free spirit, a man who'd made a new home and a new life in San Pablo, and she was a dutiful Quaker, by nature if not by religion. He belonged with someone like Stella, someone wild and free, not with an uptight little mouse of a woman who looked at him as if he were a pirate. A swashbuckler, she called him. And she was a far cry from a pirate's wench.

But he did want her. It was that simple, that basic, and it was taking all his self-control to keep from doing anything about it.

She'd finished eating, setting the metal bowl down on the dirt floor beneath her. As she moved, the unbuttoned shirt exposed a creamy expanse of breast, and he wanted to groan. He was only making things harder on himself.

She yawned, a huge, extravagant yawn that was annoyingly appealing. "I'm tired," she said.

"Yup. Hard work, kicking a Jeep over a cliff and being carried up a mountainside," he drawled, looking for trouble.

But she was too weary to deliver. "I'll replace the Jeep, of course. When we get back to Las Palmas I'll get you the money..."

"Don't worry about it. It wasn't my Jeep."

That was enough to startle her. "Whose was it?"

"No one you've met," he said, thinking of The Professor's reaction when he found out the Jeep was gone. *No one I want you to meet if I can help it.*

"How are we going to get back to Las Palmas?"

"Aren't you worried about finding your sister?"

"Can we find her?" Maggie asked. "I'm beginning to think it's a lost cause."

"I could have told you that days ago," he drawled. "She's a grown-up, you're a grown-up. Time to go your separate ways."

"But she's feckless, wild and crazy…"

"And you're responsible, sane and boring," he said.

She looked affronted. Her hair was drying in a halo of curls from the heat of the fire, and her eyes were huge and troubled. "I'm not boring."

"Your life is boring. Have you ever done one crazy, irrational thing in your entire life? Have you ever done anything that wasn't wise and well-considered and planned?" he demanded.

She bit her lip. He had a real problem with her mouth—he wanted to be there, tasting her, and her biting it only made him want it more.

She looked up at him, across the fire-lit room, over the flickering flames. "Yes," she said.

'Name it," he challenged her. "Name one stupid, crazy thing you've done in the last week, even."

"Come to San Pablo."

"That doesn't count. You were being responsible, looking out for your sister and mother."

"Okay, then. Hiring you."

He shook his head. "Not that, either. I was your only choice. And whether you want to admit it or not, you're a helluva lot better off with me than you would have been with almost anyone else. Face it, Maggie, you'd be dying of thirst and you wouldn't take a glass of water unless you'd decided it was a practical decision."

She stared at him. "I've done impractical and stupid things," she said.

"You still haven't named one."

"I kissed you."

The silence was so powerful he thought his heart had stopped beating. But it hadn't—he could feel it hammering against his chest. She wouldn't look at him—she was staring into the fire.

"So you did," he said softly. "And you never did tell me why."

She wasn't going to tell him now, either, he knew that. She wasn't even going to look at him unless he made her.

"Come over here, Maggie."

It worked. She stared at him in shock. "No."

"Don't be a baby. It's warm over here, and I've made a bed of pine boughs that should be reasonably soft. And if you want I can be on the bottom."

"Go to hell."

"Come here, Maggie. You know you want to," he said, his voice low and beguiling.

He waited, patiently, for her next heated protest. He waited for her anger, her insults, her temper. He waited, watching her, leaning back against the wall with his legs stretched out in front of him. Waited for her to come to him.

"I don't..." she began.

"Now," he said, in a firm, gentle voice.

And she came.

CHAPTER TEN

SHE DIDN'T KNOW WHY she was moving. Why she'd risen to her feet, circled the fire and come to kneel beside Ben Frazer. She had no excuse, no reason, other than she wanted to. Common sense that he'd mocked so thoroughly had vanished. The night was cool but the fire was warm, and he was there, looking at her through the smoky darkness, his blue eyes unreadable.

"I annoy you," she said in a quiet voice.

"You annoy the hell out of me," he agreed.

"Elena said you could have any woman in San Pablo."

His mouth quirked up in a half smile. "Elena's mistaken. And I don't want any woman in San Pablo."

"Don't you?"

"I want you."

She waited for him to touch her, but he didn't. He simply watched her from beneath his half-closed lids, waiting. She had no idea what he was waiting for.

"You ever sleep with a swashbuckler, Maggie?"

"No."

"You ever sleep with anyone who's not a banker?"

"No."

He looked at her. "You ever sleep with anyone at all?" he asked softly.

She didn't know what to say. The truth seemed the best idea. "Not for a long, long time."

"Define long."

"Ten years."

He closed his eyes for a moment, and she wondered if he'd send her back to her spot across the room. Then he opened them again, looking directly at her.

"Okay," he said.

"I'm not very good at this," she said, honesty compelling her. "I mean, that's sort of a given, since I haven't done it in ten years, so I'd understand if you change your mind about it—"

He stopped her babbling with his mouth. His hands caught her face, bringing it to his, and his long fingers stroked her skin. She knew an instant's panic when he pushed her mouth open with his, but there was no escape, and she didn't want to. She simply held still, letting him kiss her with a thoroughness that left her breathless and beyond any doubt of what she was getting herself into.

And then he drew back, cocking an eyebrow. "Changed your mind?" he asked softly.

"Can I?"

"Of course," he said amiably. Too amiably, as if her decision didn't matter to him in the slightest.

She started to pull back. "Then I think I'll—"

He caught her shoulders, tumbling her into his lap, and kissed her again, a slow, lazy, entirely possessive kiss that made her shiver in reluctant delight. "You think you'll what?" he whispered, calmly unfastening the tightly tied tails of the shirt she'd borrowed.

"I think I'll—"

He kissed her again, using his tongue, and she felt the shirt part beneath his hand, the one lone button still holding it together. She was sitting cradled in his lap, held there by his arms, by his mouth, by his insistent presence. She wanted to run away and hide. She wanted to push him back against the dirt floor and straddle him.

She felt the shirt pop open, heard the button go flying across the room to land somewhere in the darkness. "I'm not sewing that one on," she said when he released her mouth, though she was breathless, panting, trembling.

He was pushing the shirt from her shoulders, down her arms, and she realized she was sitting on his lap naked from the waist up. She'd never felt so exposed in her life, and instinctively she tried to cover herself with her arms.

It was a waste of time. He yanked off his own T-shirt and threw it into the darkness, and then he pulled her against his chest, and the smooth, silky warmth of his skin was irresistible. She was clutching her own bare shoulders, trying to cover herself, but he was stronger, warmer, and she wanted to touch him. She did.

"That's better, Maggie," he whispered. "Now why don't you see if you're brave enough to kiss me? You know you want to. You know I want you to. Go ahead, try it. I promise I won't bite. Or at least, not much. And only in the best possible way."

His voice was smoky and dark as the night, full of sensual possibilities, and she shivered. And she put her mouth against his, savoring the newness, the heat and damp and demand of him.

His hands slid up between them to cover her breasts, and she made a choked sound of pleasure in the back of her throat. She couldn't understand why she'd fought this, why she'd been running away from this when it felt so wonderful. And then he ran his thumbs across her nipples, and she felt a spasm between her legs, and she jerked, startled, suddenly unsure.

"Just relax, Maggie," he murmured in her ear. "I'm not going to hurt you. You'll like it, I promise you."

"I didn't before." She couldn't believe she'd actually said that out loud.

He didn't stop what he was doing, the teasing caress of his fingers on her skin, the soft temptation of his mouth on her neck. "I know. But you will this time. Trust me."

Trust me. She'd been trying to put her trust in him since she first met him, across the crowded bar in Las Cruces. He wasn't like any Boy Scout she'd ever known, he was a swashbuckling pirate, and a woman would have to be a total fool to put her trust in him.

And she was ready to be a fool. She'd fallen from her pedestal, no longer the wise Maggie Brown. She was foolish, and vulnerable and ready. And Frazer was the man who brought her to that place.

He lifted her off his lap, carefully, and set her down on the blanket. It was surprisingly soft, and he pushed her back so that she lay there, looking up at him through the flickering firelight. He reached for the waistband of her borrowed jeans, but he didn't bother unfastening it. He simply pulled the baggy pants down over her hips, off her legs, and she was naked on the soft pallet, about to curl up in a paroxysm of nerves and shyness.

She didn't have the chance. He slid over her, his body between her legs, his chest against her breasts. He was still half-dressed, and the feel of the fabric against her skin was a crazy frustration. He slid against her, the rough cloth pressing against her sensitive skin, and she couldn't stifle a hungry cry. She clutched at him, trying to pull him closer, but he simply laughed.

"Don't be in a such a hurry, sugar," he whispered. "I've got things to do." He sat back, away from her, and she closed her eyes, waiting for him to shuck off his jeans and push inside her. The sound of his zipper sent a little shiver through her, but she didn't move, waiting.

The last thing she expected was his mouth on her stomach. He trailed kisses across her skin, moving up to fasten on her breast, sucking at it like a baby, and she reached up and threaded her fingers through his long hair, holding him there, her head tipped back, her body arching with pleasure at the sensation. She'd never considered her breasts to be that sensitive, but it seemed that everywhere his mouth touched, his fingers touched, she was exquisitely responsive. She was so caught up in the pleasurable tug of his mouth on her nipple that his hand between her legs came as a surprise. And then beyond surprise, as he slid his fingers against her, and her body dissolved into a tiny shimmer of delight.

She was only half aware of what he was doing as he pulled away from her. She heard the tearing sound of a packet, and realized he was getting a condom ready. She hadn't even thought about such basics.

And then he caught her hands in his and put the condom in her palm. "Are you afraid to touch me, Maggie?" His voice was soft, raw, needy.

Very needy. She was beyond doubt, beyond fear. She slid her hand down the hard, silken length of him, and he let out a deep, guttural cry that almost made her climax again. She couldn't remember touching a man before, but the feel of him, the weight of his strength in her hand was curiously powerful, deeply erotic, and she wanted more. She wanted to taste him, take him deep in her mouth, to feel him all around her, and she started forward.

"We're too far along, Maggie," he said hoarsely. "Put the damned condom on or we'll do without it."

"I've never used one before," she said helplessly.

He cupped her hand with his, and together they pulled the thin rubber down over him. He looked like a stranger in the flickering darkness. He was a stranger, but it didn't matter. He was the only thing in the world that meant anything to her, and she lay back on the pallet and held out her arms for him.

He came to her, as strong and sure as a river, pushing her legs apart to rest against her. She felt her body spasm again, and she stared at him in shock, but he simply pushed against her, sinking slowly, inexorably, filling her. She was clutching the old blanket beneath her, and he covered her hands with his, holding tight, as he pushed all the way into her. He held still for a moment, his body rigid with self-control, as she slowly grew accustomed to the invasion. And then he reached down and pulled her legs around his narrow hips, and he began to move.

After a brief moment she relaxed, letting her body settle into the slow, delicious rhythm of his thrusts. He was right, he wouldn't hurt her, he'd already given her more pleasure than she'd even imagined. And she liked this, too, the steady, pounding pace that made her skin tingle and her heart race and her hands begin to clench against his.

He was holding her down, and she didn't like it. He was moving too slow, and she wanted faster. He was too gentle, and she wanted more, harder, and she couldn't tell him, she didn't have the words, she only knew that what had been passive and pleasant was now something that was clawing at her, tearing her apart, and she needed something she couldn't even begin to imagine.

"What do you want, Maggie?" he whispered in her ear. "What do you need?"

She wasn't going to answer. She was beyond answering, caught up in a maelstrom of need and anger, frustration and delight. She yanked her hands from under his imprisoning grip to clutch at his shoulders. He was slippery with sweat, and so was she, and she dug her fingers into his shoulder.

"What do you want, Maggie?" he whispered again, insistent. He was moving faster now, blessedly faster, pushing into her, and every time he pulled away she wanted to scream, to grab him and pull him deeper inside her.

"What do you want?"

"More," she managed in a choked voice. "You," she said. "Now."

He slid his hand between their bodies and touched her, hard, as he shoved in deep, so deep that their bodies slid across the floor to end up against the wall. The force of her climax hit her like an avalanche, and her entire body convulsed in an orgasm that was almost painful in its intensity. She could feel him in her arms, his body rigid, as he came inside her, and she wanted it to last forever, to never come back to earth, to this dark, cavelike ruin. She wanted him to stay inside her, her legs locked around him, stay like that forever. She didn't want anything else.

Her face was wet with tears. She had no idea how long it was when he lifted his head to look down at her, cupped her face and wiped the tears from her cheeks. "I forgot to bite you," he whispered. "Next time."

He was smiling at her. He was still inside her, holding her in his arms, and she felt the last little bit of doubt dissolve and vanish. "Next time," she said. And she smiled back at him.

HE GAVE THEM THEIR NIGHT. El Gallito wasn't particularly interested in sex—for him it was simply a function of the body, one his fifth wife took care of without enthusiasm or complaint. He had no interest in watching or listening to Frazer and the American.

It would have been the perfect vengeance to walk in on them at a crucial moment, but the assassin resisted the temptation. After all, he'd had a long day tracking Frazer, and he needed his rest if he was going to be any good as a marksman the next day. It wasn't as if it would be his only chance to sneak up on the two of them unawares. First light would be time enough. They'd be so worn-out they'd sleep deeply, and they wouldn't even hear his approach.

He slept in the SUV, lightly, as was his habit, waking by the first light of day. He switched on the battery and the radio of the car, searching for the first election news.

The main radio stations were state controlled, and the word all week had been of Generalissimo Cabral's upcoming victory. The powers that be would allow no less, and El Gallito, being a pragmatic man, took it with a grain of salt.

But the crackly, static-filled voice on the radio filled him with foreboding. They were discussing what would happen if the government changed hands, and El Gallito knew the situation was dire indeed.

There was no way the state-owned radio would be allowed to even hint at such a possibility unless it were already a sure thing. If Morales survived the election, Cabral was lost.

But El Gallito hadn't followed his nemesis across miles of mountainous terrain to admit defeat. He switched off the radio, turned off the battery and slid from the front seat. He'd waited long enough. Time for the two lovebirds to awaken and meet their fate.

SHE LAY IN HIS ARMS,, pale, sated, trusting. Frazer wasn't fool enough to sleep. He needed to slip away from her, get his butt down the valley to The Professor's headquarters and warn him.

They'd be packing up by now, ready to head down to the capital and claim victory. They'd be careful—The Professor had a bodyguard detail composed of the best men. Frazer should know—he trained them himself.

But they didn't know that El Gallito Loco was on the hunt. El Gallito knew this area as well as anyone—the moment they left their safe haven then Morales was a sitting duck.

She didn't wake when he slid out from beneath the covers, from the embrace of her body. He looked down at her for a long, miserable moment.

It was sex. It was good sex. No, scratch that, it was great sex. And there was no particular reason for it to have been that great. She was practically a virgin, and he was used to women who knew how to please a man and take their own pleasure. She was like a little nun, afraid of his body, afraid of her own, afraid of everything under the covers.

Ah, but she'd been easily persuaded, curious and quick to learn. He'd talked her into all sorts of things, pushing her, and she'd responded with an innocent delight that had stolen his breath, his heart, his soul.

In a different world he'd climb back under the covers and wake her, slowly, so that when she opened her eyes he'd be inside her again, and she'd smile up at him, that lazy, wicked little smile—

But this was his world, and he had responsibilities. Including abandoning her in the mountains while he saw to The Professor's safety.

He was going to have to tie her up, and she wasn't going to like it. He would have much rather have the tying up be mutual, but that wasn't in the cards. He'd send someone else to release her, probably Carlito. Carlito was six feet seven, dumb as an ox and gentle as a lamb with women. He'd take Maggie safely back to Las Palmas. Maybe by then she'd be ready to know the truth about what happened to her sister.

Or maybe they'd simply manage to get her back to the States for the time being, while the new government took charge.

She was never going to forgive him. Which was just as well—forgiveness might lead to all sorts of other things and he didn't have a hell of a lot in common with an anal retentive banker from Philadelphia.

Except the best sex of his life. And a curious, awful feeling in the pit of his stomach at the thought of never seeing her again that had absolutely nothing to do with sex and everything to do with…

Don't go there, he told himself sharply, grabbing his clothes and heading out toward the pool.

By the time he got back to the ruined room where they'd spent the night she was almost dressed. She'd found a T-shirt and the baggy pants from the night before, and she didn't look at him, busying herself with folding up the blankets.

It was what he expected. She was ashamed of the night before, embarrassed by what they'd done, wishing she'd never even met him. She probably wouldn't look him in the eye or even speak to him if she could help it, which would make his plan a lot easier. If she wasn't looking he'd be able to sneak up on her with the ropes and get her trussed up before she could try to defend herself.

Not that he'd have much difficulty. He was much stronger than she was. She had a certain resilient strength that was surprisingly erotic, though...

He had to stop thinking about it. "Good morning," he said, moving past her and reaching for the duffel bag. The ropes were coiled in one corner, and his hand found them easily.

"Morning," she muttered, concentrating on the blanket.

He held the rope behind his back, moving toward her, trying to rid himself of any thought, any emotion, any regret.

And then she looked up at him, Her eyes were huge, shadowed, her mouth soft and bruised-looking from his. She looked him straight in the eyes, and her mouth curved in a tentative, wistful smile.

"I'm in love with you," she said.

He stopped his forward pace, stunned. "Oh, hell," he said bitterly. "That's all I needed."

CHAPTER ELEVEN

IT WAS PRETTY MUCH WHAT she'd expected as a reaction to her declaration of love, Maggie thought. She didn't even know what had prompted her to announce such a thing. It was going to cause nothing but trouble, and if she'd had any sense she would have kept her mouth shut.

Problem was, she'd spent her life being sensible, and right now she wanted nothing more than to be free and irresponsible and let her emotions run wild. She was in love with him, a man she barely knew, a man who was everything she shouldn't want in a man. It was irrational, illogical and, unfortunately, true. She could deny it all she wanted, she could go back to Philadelphia and marry another banker and raise two perfect little suburban children but she'd always be in love with Ben Frazer.

She loved him enough, however, that she hated seeing the look of abject misery on his face. "Hey, don't worry about it," she said breezily, folding the blanket into a tiny, perfectly aligned square. "It's probably just postcoital bliss. Great sex tends to make a woman fanciful."

"It does." His voice was low, flat, and she didn't know whether that was an agreement or a question.

She babbled on. "You've had great sex before, so you're not likely to start thinking you're in love. I'm sure I'll get over it the moment I get back to Philadelphia. All I have to do is have sex with someone else and I'll forget all about you."

He made a low, growling noise, and she thought maybe he was grinding his teeth.

"Really, there's nothing to look so miserable about," she continued. "I've given up on finding Stella, at least for now. I'll go back home and forget all about you."

A spasm of emotion crossed his face, one she couldn't read. He took a step toward her and then stopped, his expression blank as he stared past her.

She turned and followed his gaze, and promptly dropped the blanket into the ashes of the smoldering fire.

"He knows where your sister is, *señorita*." The man was pointing a gun at both of them, a large, nasty-looking gun. "He's always known."

"Who the hell are you?" Maggie demanded. In

her entire life no one had ever pointed a gun at her. The man standing there was nondescript— middle-aged, average, the sort of man she might have passed on the street and never looked twice at. Except for his eyes. One look at his eyes told her that he was capable of absolutely anything, and she wished she'd kept her big mouth shut.

"Do you want to tell her, Frazer?" the man said. "After all, you were about to tie her up and leave her here to my tender mercies."

"Don't be ridiculous." She had enough courage left to protest that absurd statement.

But then Ben drew his hands from behind his back, and let the thin, strong rope drop to the ground. "I'd introduce you but I'm afraid I don't know his real name," Ben said in a steady voice. "He's called El Gallito Loco, roughly translated as The Crazy Chicken."

"Rooster." El Gallito corrected. "The Crazy Rooster. And I tend to think of myself as a fighting cock."

"Because he's good with razors," Ben said in an emotionless voice. "He's a killer, usually on hire to Generalissimo Cabral. Though I can't imagine why he'd come all this way just to kill me."

"Don't be naïve, Frazer. I'd cross the street to kill you, just for the sake of our past, but I wouldn't come all the way up here unless I have bigger fish to fry. No one knows where Morales is. You're going to lead me to him.''

"No." He was moving backward, toward the duffel bag, and El Gallito turned the gun on Maggie's stomach.

"Don't bother looking for your guns, Frazer. I took the liberty of removing them while you were otherwise occupied.''

"You carry a gun?'' Maggie demanded, shocked.

"He can be quite lethal himself, *señorita.* Your intrepid guide happens to be Ramon Morales de Lorca y Antonio's right hand man. In charge of security, in charge of training his bodyguards. I still can't figure out why he's dragged you all over the country instead of simply silencing you, but then, Americans are ever a puzzle.''

"Who?''

"Better known as The Professor. The man who will be the leader of San Pablo unless I do something about it,'' the stranger said.

"And you really think I'd take you to him?'' Ben countered. "You've lived longer than that, pal. I'd gladly die before turning him over to you.''

"Yes, I know. But would you let me kill the girl?''

Ben didn't even look at her. Didn't even hesitate. "Of course."

"I don't think The Professor's mistress will be too pleased with that."

Frazer shrugged. "That won't be my problem, now will it? You'll kill us both."

"What's The Professor got to do with this?" Maggie demanded.

"Shut up, Maggie!" Frazer snapped.

"She doesn't know, does she? While you were dragging her on a wild-goose chase and humping her bones she never had the faintest idea that her sister's been happily living with the man who wants to be president of San Pablo."

"Ramon?" Maggie breathed.

"Ramon Morales de Lorca y Antonio. The Professor."

"He's not her type," she protested.

"When it comes to true love there's no such thing as type," the stranger said.

"Now who would have pegged you for a romantic?" Frazer drawled.

"Oh, I'm a very romantic fellow. I intend to make sure both The Professor and his American girlfriend die together, so they can spend eternity at each other's side. I wish I could do the same for you two, but she's a liability."

"So am I. I'm not giving him up."

He was a paunchy old man, but lightning fast on his feet. Before Maggie realized what he was doing he'd crossed the room and caught her in an iron grip, and she could feel the cold steel of the gun pressed beneath her breast.

Frazer was frozen, unmoving. And then he shrugged. "Kill her. It won't make any difference. The people of San Pablo are worth one innocent American life."

El Gallito put a meaty hand on her shoulder and shoved her to her knees. She could feel the cold steel at the back of her neck, and bile rose in her throat. She didn't want to die, and she most particularly didn't want to die vomiting.

She heard the cock of the gun, and she squeezed her eyes shut, holding her breath, stupidly, when it would be her last breath. She was going to die, and Ben Frazer was going to stand there and let it happen. The silence would be broken by the blast of a gun, and then it would end, everything.

"Don't."

The moment had stretched into an endless eternity, broken at the last possible moment by Ben's voice. Maggie let out her pent-up breath in a silent *whoosh*.

"You'll take me to The Professor?"

"Yes."

"You won't make the mistake of calling out and warning him, now would you? Because then I'd have to kill her anyway, and you would have gained nothing."

"I'll take you to him, but you'll leave her behind. She'd just slow us down," Ben said, his voice cool and emotionless. She looked at him, still on her knees in the dirt, but he was staring straight ahead.

"She comes with us. She's my only guarantee that you'll do as you promise."

"And then what?"

El Gallito smiled, a perfect, feral smile. "You know I'll try to kill you. But I'll be much more concerned about The Professor and his girlfriend. If you're lucky you'll get away. But I'd leave the country if I were you. Generalissimo Cabral is not happy about coming so close to losing power, and he'll make it his goal to wipe out any last bits of support for The Professor. And I imagine The Professor's people won't be happy that you turned traitor." He sighed happily. "No, maybe I won't kill you. Destroying your life would be much better."

"Still can't get over the fact that I beat you. Twice," Frazer taunted him.

El Gallito's smile vanished. "A fluke. But this day's work will more than make up for it. On your feet, *señorita*. We have an appointment to keep."

THEY WALKED SINGLE FILE, following the narrow pathway. Ben went first, leading the way, not daring to look back at either Maggie or El Gallito. He was still sweating in the cool mountain air.

He'd survived more than thirty years living on his instincts. His instincts had told him that El Gallito wouldn't kill Maggie, not yet, and he'd risked her life on that instinct. He'd won, but it had been a close call, and once El Gallito had put the barrel of the handgun at the base of her skull he'd known he was caught.

He shouldn't have caved in. If El Gallito had executed her he'd have no more bargaining power to make Ben do what he wanted him to, and the assassin was too smart a man to make a mistake like that.

But in the end, Ben couldn't risk it. Couldn't risk Maggie, even though logic told him that the needs of the many outweigh the needs of the few. He couldn't let her go.

She hadn't spoken to him, looked at him, since El Gallito had hauled her to her feet. And there had been nothing he could say, particularly with the assassin watching her. He'd used her, betrayed her, made her trust him and then destroyed that trust. And now he was probably going to end up getting her killed as well.

What was there he could say that would make it better?

He knew the answer, much as he wanted to avoid it. The plain, unpleasant, unvarnished truth that he didn't want to admit.

They were nearing the divide, where the paths converged and led down into the hidden valley. There was always the possibility that everyone had already packed up and left, but he didn't think so. The plans had been made weeks ago, and The Professor wasn't the kind of man to let fear influence him. He would do what he'd decided to do, and to hell with the forces of darkness that tried to stop him.

He could hear the faint rasp of her breathing behind him, but she didn't say a word. She had to be exhausted—she wasn't used to the terrain or the altitude, nor, he expected, the hard work. She was a city woman, a banker, not used to scrambling over rocks.

The brush was still covering the split rock, and he pushed it out of the way, exposing the entrance.

"Very clever," El Gallito said behind them. "I would have searched for days without finding it."

Ben turned, blocking the way. "Why don't you leave us behind here? He's down there—The Professor and most of his company. There's no other way in—I can't warn him, and he'll be a sitting duck. Maggie and I will just hold you back."

"Kind of you to be worried about me, but I think we'll just keep on," El Gallito said. "She may have been fool enough to trust you, but I'm not so innocent."

She wouldn't look at him, wouldn't look at either of them. He could see the absolute weariness and fear radiating from her. "I need a break," he said abruptly. "Give me a few minutes to rest."

El Gallito's wry grin was far from reassuring. "Your lady-friend can have a rest, Frazer. You can even sit with her and whisper sweet nothings. I have nothing to fear. I'm the one with the gun, and I'm not troubled by moral or ethical concerns, thank God."

Without another word Maggie collapsed on a rock, her head bowed. El Gallito was true to his word, keeping his distance, and Ben approached her, determined to say the words.

She looked up as he drew near, her gaze murderous. "Don't even try it," she said. "I'll let him shoot me before I talk to you."

"Don't be an idiot. There's a chance we can get out of this if we work together," he growled, keeping his voice low.

"Maybe I'd rather die," she shot back.

"Well, I wouldn't. He's going to be watching us pretty closely and we probably won't have another chance to talk. Our best chance will be when we come in sight of the encampment. Once he starts looking for Ramon he'll forget about us, at least for the moment. When I give the word I want you to hit the dirt."

"Yeah, sure," she said. "I'll put my life in your hands, why not?"

"You don't have any other choice. I saved your life back there. I'll save it again if you don't annoy me." His voice was cool and clipped, conveying none of the crazed emotions that were churning beneath him.

"I should be so lucky. What's the word?"

"What word?"

"How you're going to warn me?" she prompted with the patience of a saint to an idiot.

"How about bitch?"

"It'll do," she said sweetly.

"Let's get moving," El Gallito called from his spot a few yards away.

"Oh, and one more thing," Ben whispered.

"What?"

"I love you, too."

She kicked him in the shin.

His limp didn't make progress any faster, and he exaggerated it just enough to slow them down more. El Gallito soon lost his amusement over the situation and began shoving Maggie in the back, the one tactic that would make Frazer pick up his feet. He glanced at his watch in disbelief. It wasn't yet ten in the morning, yet they'd been walking for hours.

There were birds wheeling and calling overhead, and he knew what they'd find just over the next rise. Every muscle in his body tensed. El Gallito's gun didn't have a silencer, but he was a man who was far too handy with a razor, and he could cut Maggie's throat before Ben even turned around. All he could think to do was throw himself backward when the time came, knocking her out of harm's way. It was a weak plan, but the only thing he could come up with at the spur-of-the-moment.

He heard the music first, and he stifled a miserable groan. What rotten timing, on top of everything else! The guitars and flutes floated over the treetops on a gentle breeze, and overhead the sun was shining. It was much too beautiful a day to die.

"What's that?" El Gallito demanded.

Ben halted, just a few yards away from the outcropping that would display everything, and Maggie barreled into him. When she realized she was touching him she put her hands out to shove him away, and it was easy enough to scoot her around behind him while he concentrated on distracting El Gallito.

"What do you think it is?" he replied. "That's the problem with you *nationalistas*—no imagination."

El Gallito's bleak eyes narrowed. "The fool isn't getting married!"

"Sounds like it to me."

"Married? Who?" Maggie echoed. Before he could stop her she crossed the last few yards to the outcropping, with Ben and El Gallito just seconds beyond her.

Ben only had time to take in the tableau. The priest, the tall, balding bridegroom, the very pregnant bride. And then Maggie shrieked her sister's name. "Stella!"

It was enough to startle El Gallito. Ben was on him before he could fire the gun, and the shot went wild, disappearing into the trees. "Run, damn it," he shouted over his shoulder as he struggled with the assassin's fierce strength. He'd faced his razors before, but he'd been armed himself, and even so he still had the scars to prove it. The outcome wasn't nearly so optimistic this time.

He could hear the shouts from the valley, and he knew Ramon's men would be there in moments, though he wasn't quite sure whether he had moments or not. El Gallito had a ten-inch-long razor in one hand, and he was using all his force to bring it closer, closer to his throat. One second of weakness and he'd slash his jugular. He really didn't want to bleed to death in the mountains, just when Ramon had accomplished what they'd worked so hard for.

Then again, he'd told Maggie he loved her and gotten kicked for his troubles. Maybe he'd be better off dead.

The blade was moving closer, closer to his neck. He was stronger than El Gallito, younger, but part of his concentration was on Maggie. "Get... the...hell...out of here!" he wheezed, wondering if they were going to be his last words.

And then El Gallito collapsed on top of him in a dead heap. The razor was caught between their bodies, and he felt it nick his throat before it fell to the ground. He looked up, and Maggie was standing over them, a huge rock in her hand. There was blood on the rock, and he realized she must have clobbered El Gallito with it.

The assassin was either unconscious or dead, and Ben didn't really care which. He shoved his body aside, just as Maggie dropped the heavy rock and brushed her hands clean.

"Now we're even," she said to Frazer. And then she turned to face her long lost, almost married, very pregnant sister.

CHAPTER TWELVE

MAGGIE BROWN WAS NOT in a very good mood, considering it was her sister's wedding day, she was about to become an aunt, and feckless Stella had finally found someone worth sticking with. Ramon Morales de Lorca y Antonio was a far cry from the romantic revolutionary Maggie had been imagining. Tall, stoop-shouldered, balding and bespectacled, he looked just like his nickname, The Professor. And Stella, silly, romantic, changeable Stella, was obviously, deeply, desperately in love for the first time in her life.

"I can't believe you're really here!" she cried, flinging her arms around Maggie and pressing her against her huge, pregnant belly. "I told Ramon I wouldn't marry him unless my family could come to the wedding, but then when the little one started acting like he was going to make an early appearance I decided I was being silly. When Mother said you were already here I kept waiting for you to show up, but then Ramon said Ben was looking after you and I figured, hey, who better to look after my twin sister than the stud of San Pablo? Not that he's really a stud—he hasn't had a woman in more than a year, Ramon says. He's looking for the right woman, which I highly doubt because even though Ramon is the kind of man who wants to settle down, I don't think Ben will ever be.''

"You talked with Mother?" Maggie broke through the stream of consciousness that was Stella's usual mode of conversation to get to what was important. And anyway, she hadn't the slightest interest in anything her sister had to say about Ben Frazer.

"Called her a couple of days ago," Stella said blithely. "Would you ever have thought I'd be so settled down and maternal? I've even stopped smoking—Ramon says it's no good for the baby and besides, how would it look for the First Lady to be a smoker when Ramon is so hot on health issues? For that matter, can you imagine me as a First Lady of a country, even one as tiny as San Pablo? I can't believe—"

"How is she?"

"How is who?" Stella said blankly.

"Mother. I tried to call her but there was no answer. She's been very sick, and I was afraid—"

"Maggie!" Stella said. "Don't tell me you believed her when she told you she was dying? She does that anytime she's not getting her own way. I've been used to it for years. She's as strong as a horse. She wanted to come to the wedding but I told her she couldn't choose my china pattern. I don't even know if I'll have a china pattern. Anyway, she decided to stay in Las Vegas and come over for the inauguration. I figure I'll surprise her with the christening. Didn't want to dump too much on her at one time."

"Las Vegas?" Maggie was getting dizzy.

"You remember Uncle Joe, don't you? Of course, he wasn't really our uncle, and he and Mother were always good friends. Well, his wife died a few months ago, so he showed up at Mother's door asking her to go to Las Vegas with him and she said yes. I wouldn't be surprised if she marries him."

Maggie sat down abruptly, her head spinning. "I'm not taking all this in," she said faintly.

"Well, of course not, darling. You've had a tough time, what with being cooped up with Ben for days and then running into that Chicken Man. I don't blame you for being upset. But all's well that ends well, and you can be my maid of honor. Though we're going to have to hurry."

"Why?" Maggie asked, half afraid of the answer.

Stella smiled at her brightly. "Because I'm in labor."

In retrospect it was just as well that Delia hadn't made it to her daughter's wedding, Maggie thought later. There were three ceremonies in a row—a civil ceremony, a Catholic ceremony and a long, convoluted traditional San Pablo ceremony that went entirely over Maggie's head as she held her sister's hands and helped her breathe. Fortunately the priest who conducted all three ceremonies was also a medic, and Ramon Benjamino was born moments after the last vows had been concluded.

Her new brother-in-law wept tears of joy as he held his new son. His best man, Ben Frazer, kept his distance, and if Maggie felt his eyes on her she did her best to ignore him. Stella was looking, as usual, radiant, and she'd come through the quick labor and delivery with nothing more than some loud screams and a few pungent curses, which the priest graciously ignored. She took one celebratory sip of wine and promptly fell asleep nursing her newborn.

And then there was no one to turn to. Except Ben, looking at her from across the compound. Only a hundred or so strangers between her and him, not enough to cause a real distraction, and he looked as if he was going to come after her, and if he did she wasn't sure if she could handle it.

"I want to thank you for all that you did." Her new brother-in-law was by her side, speaking to her in halting English. "I deeply regret that you weren't brought here sooner, but we were worried you would try to talk Stella out of marrying me."

"We?" She tore her gaze away from Ben. "You and Stella?"

Ramon shook his head. "Stella told me I was being foolish. Ben thought it would be best to keep you far away from here, and I agreed. In retrospect I can see there was no need, but we thought it better to be careful. I knew you'd be in good hands with Ben, and this place has been a well-kept secret. We really couldn't afford to let you come here until we were ready to leave."

We, again. Ben and Ramon. She glanced back at Frazer. "I need to get home," she said abruptly.

"But Stella was hoping you could stay for a while. It is going to be a difficult time for her, and she could use a sister…"

"I've been away from my work too long," Maggie said. "I'll come back and visit later, after she's settled."

Ramon didn't look happy, but unlike his cohort

he wasn't the sort of man to force his own way. "Very well," he said. "I'll have Ben drive you to Las Palmas—"

"No!" Her protest was loud enough to make several heads turn her way, including Ben's. "Someone else, please," she said in a softer voice.

Ramon's high forehead wrinkled in worry. "Has he offered you any insult? Frazer is my closest friend and adviser, but I would hate to think he'd offended my new sister—"

"No offense," she said swiftly. "He's just been dragging me around this country for days. I'm sure he'd prefer to stay and help you move back to the capital. You must have need of him. And I'd just as soon have...someone else drive me."

"If you wish," Ramon said reluctantly. "Father Gades is heading back to the city tonight, and he will be glad to take you. Word has come that Generalissimo Cabral has left the country, and the good father wants to pave the way for our arrival. Still, I am concerned for your safety."

"There's nothing to worry about. You've got El Gallito tied up, and if the *Generalissimo* has conceded then everything will be fine."

"But I don't..." At that moment his wife awoke, and while he was distracted Maggie slipped away. Before he could come up with one more argument. Before Stella could beg her to stay. Before she took one more look at her brand-new nephew and melted.

Before she had to see Ben Frazer again.

Father Gades spoke very little English, which Maggie considered her first lucky break. She waited until they were safely out of the encampment before she curled up on the seat to sleep. There had been no sign of Ben. He was probably out celebrating his close call, thanking God he didn't even have to say goodbye to her. It was over, the whole dangerous, deceitful, embarrassing mess, and if she ever returned to San Pablo she'd be in complete control of her life and her emotions.

It seemed likely that sooner or later she was going to have to come back. Stella was in love, with a husband, with a baby, with a country. Stella didn't need her twin sister watching out for her anymore. If she ever really had needed her.

Maybe Frazer was right about one thing. Maybe it was time to start taking care of herself.

She awoke suddenly, disoriented, and for a moment she'd forgotten where she was. The priest's black sedan had come to a stop, and he was looking at her expectantly. Maggie peered out the window at the tiny airport. She'd made it. And Ben Frazer hadn't followed her.

Father Gades gave her a long, graceful speech, and while she recognized El Gallito Loco and Frazer, few of the other words made any sense. So she simply smiled and nodded, patting the priest's hand as he continued to talk to her. Maybe he was looking for a convert, she thought. Or maybe he was just trying to save her soul.

He was still talking when she climbed out of the car and shut the door behind her. Finally he gave up, putting the car into gear and driving away, leaving her alone in the lamplight outside the one low building that comprised Las Palmas International Airport.

And that was when she remembered that her money, her credit cards and her passport were at the bottom of a cliff in the back of a ruined Jeep.

The priest had already disappeared, and she had no choice but to enter the airport. Surely they had some kind of help, travelers' aid or something. Since the U.S. government wasn't on particularly friendly terms with Generalissimo Cabral there was no embassy in San Pablo, but there must be someone she could turn to for help. Hell, she was the president-elect's sister-in-law. Someone would come to her aid.

The airport terminal was a madhouse, people rushing around, voices high-pitched and shrill. It was several minutes before she could even get someone to listen to her, even longer before she tracked down someone who spoke English.

"No more planes tonight, *señorita*," the harried man said. "Every plane in San Pablo has left."

"But why?"

"Generalissimo Cabral, his family, his supporters and his personal bodyguard have commandeered every available jet, plane and helicopter. The General himself left more than an hour ago, and the last plane is taking off even as we speak. I can only suggest you find a hotel room for the night. By tomorrow the planes will return, and we will do our best to get you out on the first one."

"But I've lost my purse," she said for what seemed like the seventeenth time. "My passport, my money, my credit cards..."

"That is a great deal too bad, *señorita*, but I'm afraid I can be of no assistance in this matter," the man said hurriedly. "There are a few of Generalissimo Cabral's men left behind. Perhaps they can help you."

"Er...no thanks," she said, backing away. If worse came to worst she could find her way back to the old section of town and throw herself on Elena's mercy.

"Wait a minute, *señorita*," the man called after

her, but she kept moving, until she came up against a solid, immovable form.

She froze. He smelled like garlic and stale flesh and dried blood. It couldn't be. But it was.

"Señorita Brown," said the man she knew only as El Gallito Loco. He had a soiled bandage on his head, his neat suit was bloodstained, and his empty eyes were even more terrifying. "How fortunate that we happened to meet up."

She opened her mouth to scream when she felt the barrel of the gun against her side. "Don't make a noise and embarrass yourself, lady," he said in her ear, his voice hoarse. "These men won't help you. They've abandoned the *Generalissimo,* but they haven't yet formed an allegiance to Morales. And one lone American woman isn't of much importance in the midst of the revolution. You just come along quietly."

She held still. "Why should I?" she countered. "You're just going to kill me."

"Maybe not. Maybe I'll use you to lure Frazer back. I can't save the *Generalissimo,* but I have an old score to settle. With Frazer, and with you. You might have broken my skull. Fortunately I have a hard head. It takes a lot to kill a man like me, *señorita.* You didn't even come close."

"Sorry," she said briefly. "I should have used more force."

His hand tightened on her arm, biting into her flesh so that she bit back a yelp of pain. No one was watching. El Gallito was right—there was too much panic and confusion for anyone to pay much attention to one lone woman.

"Come along," he said again, dragging her. And she had no choice but to stumble along with him as he pulled her toward the exit. Not the front exit, with the lights, but off to the side, where there would be no witnesses.

She wasn't going to make it out alive, she told herself. She'd survived almost certain death at least twice already—this time her luck had run out.

He pushed her through the door, so hard that she sprawled on the concrete. It took her a moment to scramble to her feet, but the gun was out now, pointing straight at her.

"You're going to kill me, aren't you?" she said calmly. "I should have made you do it in there. Then at least you wouldn't get away with it."

"I always get away with it, *señorita,*" he said politely. "A half-dozen witnesses make little difference. I'll be following the *Generalissimo* first thing tomorrow morning, but first I need to take care of a little business."

"I thought you wanted to kill Frazer, not me."

"Ah, but then I thought about it, and I decided it would be far more painful for Frazer to have to live, knowing his carelessness brought your death, than to kill him. Death is instantaneous, and I want him to suffer."

"He's not going to give a damn if you kill me. Morales might be pissed off, but Ben won't care."

"That's where you're wrong, sweetheart."

The voice came out of the darkness, shocking in its suddenness, and El Gallito swerved around, firing wildly toward the sound.

Three shots, and all she could do was flatten herself back on the pavement and cover her head. If she was going to die then so be it, but she wasn't going to make an easy target.

The silence was deafening. She uncovered her head and peered up, to see El Gallito looming over her, swaying slightly, his eyes empty. And then he pitched forward onto the pavement beside her, dead.

She scrambled away from him in a mindless panic, only to be brought up in Ben Frazer's strong arms. She stared up at him, wild-eyed. "You killed him," she said.

"Yes." His electric-blue eyes were opaque, unreadable.

She wanted to stand on her own, but her legs were trembling so much that she could barely keep upright. His hands were holding her, and she liked it, needed it, even more than she hated him.

"How did he escape?" she asked in a shaky voice.

"I didn't know that he had."

"Then why are you here?"

"We have some unfinished business."

"Oh, no, we don't..." she protested fiercely, but he simply picked her up in his arms.

"Can we continue this conversation somewhere other than beside El Gallito's body?" he asked in a sardonic voice. "I haven't killed that many men in my life and he gives me the willies."

"Don't you need to do something about him?"

"Someone will clean up the mess later," he said carelessly. "It's not like it hasn't happened before in Generalissimo Cabral's San Pablo."

She didn't bother arguing. They got as far as the roadway, and she recognized the Jeep. "I thought I crashed it," she said.

"The Professor has more than one. Not that he wanted to trust me with it, after what happened to the last one. But when he heard I was coming after you he agreed."

"You were coming after me," she said stiffly.

He set her down, carefully. She took a step back from him, because she needed to stand on her own two feet. He looked wary, uncertain, staring down at her.

"Your sister wants you to stay," he said. "She needs you. She's got too much on her plate, and she needs your help."

"I don't need to take care of her anymore, didn't you tell me that? She's twenty-eight years old, she can stand on her own two feet."

"She doesn't need you to take care of her. She just needs help," he said. "And The Professor, he needs you. You can help him understand the world financial situation..."

"I'm a banker from Philadelphia, not a secretary of the treasury, for heaven's sake!" she shot back.

His half grin would have been endearing if she didn't want to kick him again. "You never know what the future holds. You know more about money than Ramon does, that's for sure."

"So I'm supposed to stay and help out my sister and brother-in-law?"

"And the country. There's a lot of work to be done now that the *Generalissimo* has left. He's been stripping this place bare for the past thirty years. We need all the help we can get to put it back together."

"And what will you be doing?"

He shrugged. "Anything I can."

"I'm sure you'll be fine," she said briskly. "San Pablo has survived without me before and it'll do very well without me in the future."

"Ramon needs me."

"So?" she said coolly.

"I'm not going to be any good to him in Philadelphia. Besides, whoever heard of a swashbuckler in Philadelphia?"

She stared at him. "What are you talking about?"

"I lied to you, I tricked you, and I was ready to tie you up and leave you. I took advantage of you time and time again."

"And?"

"And..." He took a deep, painful breath. "I'm sorry. Damn, I hate apologizing," he added bitterly.

She could feel the first embers of hope begin to glow in the pit of her stomach. "Apology accepted," she said coolly. "And now I've got a plane to catch." She started to walk away from him, knowing there was no plane, knowing she had no passport nor money to get one.

He caught her arm, just as she knew he would.

Her back was toward him, so he couldn't see the sudden smile that blazed across her face.

"You don't want to be a pirate wench in Philadelphia, Maggie," he said. "Stay here."

She schooled her features, then turned to look at him. "Stay here and be a banker?" she questioned with deceptive calm.

"Stay here and love me."

A slow, sure smile lit her face. Delia would get to choose a china pattern after all. "Frazer," she said, "you're going to hate my mother." And she went into his arms, home at last.

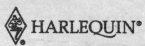

HARLEQUIN®
INTRIGUE

IS *THE* PLACE
FOR BREATHTAKING
ROMANTIC SUSPENSE!

Harlequin Intrigue brings you all that you
want in category romance—and more!
Four titles each month deliver the drama
of romance *plus* an explosive sense of
suspense for a thrilling reading experience
that will leave you breathless.
From whodunits to witness protection,
you get variety and the guarantee of
a happy ending—case closed!

So unlock the mystery of the heart
with Harlequin Intrigue.
You won't be disappointed.

HARLEQUIN®
Makes any time special ™

MIRA Books® publishes
the brightest stars in fiction,
and now, the incomparable

ANNE STUART

She's sexy...She's sinister...
And she's defined her own genre
of contemporary gothics!

Hypnotic and alluring—that's the hallmark of an
Anne Stuart novel. Over the years this one-of-a-kind
author has assembled a devoted following of readers
utterly mesmerized by her unique brand of storytelling.
So seductive, no one can read just one. Fortunately, we
have your Anne Stuart fix covered. All you have to do is
surrender to the darker side of romance.

You can also find Anne Stuart titles from
Harlequin American Romance® and Harlequin Intrigue®.

Too much is never enough!

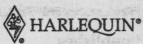

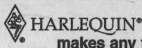